Lucretia P. Hale

The Last of the Peterkins

Lucretia P. Hale

The Last of the Peterkins

1st Edition | ISBN: 978-3-75236-309-8

Place of Publication: Frankfurt am Main, Germany

Year of Publication: 2020

Outlook Verlag GmbH, Germany.

THE LAST OF THE PETERKINS,

With Others of their kin.

BY LUCRETIA P. HALE.

PREFACE.

The following Papers contain the last records of the Peterkin Family, who unhappily ventured to leave their native land and have never returned. Elizabeth Eliza's Commonplace Book has been found among the family papers, and will be published here for the first time. It is evident that she foresaw that the family were ill able to contend with the commonplace struggle of life; and we may not wonder that they could not survive the unprecedented, far away from the genial advice of friends, especially that of the Lady from Philadelphia.

It is feared that Mr. and Mrs. Peterkin lost their lives after leaving Tobolsk, perhaps in some vast conflagration.

Agamemnon and Solomon John were probably sacrificed in some effort to join in or control the disturbances which arose in the distant places where they had established themselves,—Agamemnon in Madagascar, Solomon John in Rustchuk.

The little boys have merged into men in some German university, while Elizabeth Eliza must have been lost in the mazes of the Russian language.

I.

ELIZABETH ELIZA WRITES A PAPER.

Elizabeth Eliza joined the Circumambient Club with the idea that it would be a long time before she, a new member, would have to read a paper. She would have time to hear the other papers read, and to see how it was done; and she would find it easy when her turn came. By that time she would have some ideas; and long before she would be called upon, she would have leisure to sit down and write out something. But a year passed away, and the time was drawing near. She had, meanwhile, devoted herself to her studies, and had tried to inform herself on all subjects by way of preparation. She had consulted one of the old members of the Club as to the choice of a subject.

"Oh, write about anything," was the answer,—"anything you have been thinking of."

Elizabeth Eliza was forced to say she had not been thinking lately. She had not had time. The family had moved, and there was always an excitement about something, that prevented her sitting down to think.

"Why not write out your family adventures?" asked the old member.

Elizabeth Eliza was sure her mother would think it made them too public; and most of the Club papers, she observed, had some thought in them. She preferred to find an idea.

ELIZABETH ELIZA WRITES A PAPER.

So she set herself to the occupation of thinking. She went out on the piazza to think; she stayed in the house to think. She tried a corner of the china-closet. She tried thinking in the cars, and lost her pocket-book; she tried it in the garden, and walked into the strawberry bed. In the house and out of the house, it seemed to be the same,—she could not think of anything to think of. For many weeks she was seen sitting on the sofa or in the window, and nobody disturbed her. "She is thinking about her paper," the family would say, but she only knew that she could not think of anything.

Agamemnon told her that many writers waited till the last moment, when inspiration came which was much finer than anything studied. Elizabeth Eliza thought it would be terrible to wait till the last moment, if the inspiration

4

should not come! She might combine the two ways,—wait till a few days before the last, and then sit down and write anyhow. This would give a chance for inspiration, while she would not run the risk of writing nothing.

She was much discouraged. Perhaps she had better give it up? But, no; everybody wrote a paper: if not now, she would have to do it sometime!

And at last the idea of a subject came to her! But it was as hard to find a moment to write as to think. The morning was noisy, till the little boys had gone to school; for they had begun again upon their regular course, with the plan of taking up the study of cider in October. And after the little boys had gone to school, now it was one thing, now it was another,—the china-closet to be cleaned, or one of the neighbors in to look at the sewing-machine. She tried after dinner, but would fall asleep. She felt that evening would be the true time, after the cares of day were over.

The Peterkins had wire mosquito-nets all over the house,—at every door and every window. They were as eager to keep out the flies as the mosquitoes. The doors were all furnished with strong springs, that pulled the doors to as soon as they were opened. The little boys had practised running in and out of each door, and slamming it after them. This made a good deal of noise, for they had gained great success in making one door slam directly after another, and at times would keep up a running volley of artillery, as they called it, with the slamming of the doors. Mr. Peterkin, however, preferred it to flies.

So Elizabeth Eliza felt she would venture to write of a summer evening with all the windows open.

She seated herself one evening in the library, between two large kerosene lamps, with paper, pen, and ink before her. It was a beautiful night, with the smell of the roses coming in through the mosquito-nets, and just the faintest odor of kerosene by her side. She began upon her work. But what was her dismay! She found herself immediately surrounded with mosquitoes. They attacked her at every point. They fell upon her hand as she moved it to the inkstand; they hovered, buzzing, over her head; they planted themselves under the lace of her sleeve. If she moved her left hand to frighten them off from one point, another band fixed themselves upon her right hand. Not only did they flutter and sting, but they sang in a heathenish manner, distracting her attention as she tried to write, as she tried to waft them off. Nor was this all. Myriads of June-bugs and millers hovered round, flung themselves into the lamps, and made disagreeable funeral-pyres of themselves, tumbling noisily on her paper in their last unpleasant agonies. Occasionally one darted with a rush toward Elizabeth Eliza's head.

If there was anything Elizabeth Eliza had a terror of, it was a June-bug. She had heard that they had a tendency to get into the hair. One had been caught in the hair of a friend of hers, who had long luxuriant hair. But the legs of the June-bug were caught in it like fish-hooks, and it had to be cut out, and the June-bug was only extricated by sacrificing large masses of the flowing locks.

Elizabeth Eliza flung her handkerchief over her head. Could she sacrifice what hair she had to the claims of literature? She gave a cry of dismay.

The little boys rushed in a moment to the rescue. They flapped newspapers, flung sofa-cushions; they offered to stand by her side with fly-whisks, that she might be free to write. But the struggle was too exciting for her, and the flying insects seemed to increase. Moths of every description—large brown moths, small, delicate white millers—whirled about her, while the irritating hum of the mosquito kept on more than ever. Mr. Peterkin and the rest of the family came in to inquire about the trouble. It was discovered that each of the little boys had been standing in the opening of a wire door for some time, watching to see when Elizabeth Eliza would have made her preparations and would begin to write. Countless numbers of dorbugs and winged creatures of every description had taken occasion to come in. It was found that they were in every part of the house.

"We might open all the blinds and screens," suggested Agamemnon, "and make a vigorous onslaught and drive them all out at once."

"I do believe there are more inside than out now," said Solomon John.

"The wire nets, of course," said Agamemnon, "keep them in now."

"We might go outside," proposed Solomon John, "and drive in all that are left. Then to-morrow morning, when they are all torpid, kill them and make collections of them."

Agamemnon had a tent which he had provided in case he should ever go to the Adirondacks, and he proposed using it for the night. The little boys were wild for this.

Mrs. Peterkin thought she and Elizabeth Eliza would prefer trying to sleep in the house. But perhaps Elizabeth Eliza would go on with her paper with more comfort out of doors.

A student's lamp was carried out, and she was established on the steps of the back piazza, while screens were all carefully closed to prevent the mosquitoes and insects from flying out. But it was of no use. There were outside still swarms of winged creatures that plunged themselves about her, and she had not been there long before a huge miller flung himself into the lamp and put it out. She gave up for the evening.

Still the paper went on. "How fortunate," exclaimed Elizabeth Eliza, "that I did not put it off till the last evening!" Having once begun, she persevered in it at every odd moment of the day. Agamemnon presented her with a volume of "Synonymes," which was of great service to her. She read her paper, in its various stages, to Agamemnon first, for his criticism, then to her father in the library, then to Mr. and Mrs. Peterkin together, next to Solomon John, and afterward to the whole family assembled. She was almost glad that the lady from Philadelphia was not in town, as she wished it to be her own unaided production. She declined all invitations for the week before the night of the club, and on the very day she kept her room with *eau sucrée*, that she might save her voice. Solomon John provided her with Brown's Bronchial Troches when the evening came, and Mrs. Peterkin advised a handkerchief over her head, in case of June-bugs. It was, however, a cool night. Agamemnon escorted her to the house.

The Club met at Ann Maria Bromwick's. No gentlemen were admitted to the regular meetings. There were what Solomon John called "occasional annual meetings," to which they were invited, when all the choicest papers of the year were re-read.

Elizabeth Eliza was placed at the head of the room, at a small table, with a brilliant gas-jet on one side. It was so cool the windows could be closed. Mrs. Peterkin, as a guest, sat in the front row.

This was her paper, as Elizabeth Eliza read it, for she frequently inserted fresh expressions:—

THE SUN.

It is impossible that much can be known about it. This is why we have taken it up as a subject. We mean the sun that lights us by day and leaves us by night. In the first place, it is so far off. No measuring-tapes could reach it; and both the earth and the sun are moving about so, that it would be difficult to adjust ladders to reach it, if we could. Of course, people have written about it, and there are those who have told us how many miles off it is. But it is a very large number, with a great many figures in it; and though it is taught in most if not all of our public schools, it is a chance if any one of the scholars remembers exactly how much it is.

It is the same with its size. We cannot, as we have said, reach it by ladders to measure it; and if we did reach it, we should have no measuring-tapes large enough, and those that shut up with springs are difficult to use in a high place. We are told, it is true, in a great many of the school-books, the size of the sun; but, again, very few of those who have learned the number have been able to remember it after they have recited it, even if they remembered it then. And almost all of the scholars have lost their school-books, or have neglected to carry them home, and so they are not able to refer to them,—I mean, after leaving school. I must say that is the case with me, I should say with us, though it was different. The older ones gave their school-books to the younger ones, who took them back to school to lose them, or who have destroyed them when there were no younger ones to go to school. I should say there are such families. What I mean is, the fact that in some families there are no younger children to take off the school-books. But even then they are put away on upper shelves, in closets or in attics, and seldom found if wanted,—if then, dusty.

Of course, we all know of a class of persons called astronomers, who might be able to give us information on the subject in hand, and who probably do furnish what information is found in school-books. It should be observed, however, that these astronomers carry on their observations always in the night. Now, it is well known that the sun does not shine in the night. Indeed, that is one of the peculiarities of the night, that there is no sun to light us, so we have to go to bed as long as there is nothing else we can do without its light, unless we use lamps, gas, or kerosene, which is very well for the evening, but would be expensive all night long; the same with candles. How, then, can we depend upon their statements, if not made from their own observation?—I mean, if they never saw the sun?

We cannot expect that astronomers should give us any valuable information with regard to the sun, which they never see, their occupation compelling them to be up at night. It is quite likely that they never see it; for we should not expect them to sit up all day as well as all night, as, under such circumstances, their lives would not last long.

Indeed, we are told that their name is taken from the word *aster*, which means "star;" the word is "aster—know—more." This, doubtless, means that they know more about the stars than other things. We see, therefore, that their knowledge is confined to the stars, and we cannot trust what they have to tell us of the sun.

There are other asters which should not be mixed up with these,—we mean those growing by the wayside in the fall of the year. The astronomers, from their nocturnal habits, can scarcely be acquainted with them; but as it does not come within our province, we will not inquire.

We are left, then, to seek our own information about the sun. But we are met with a difficulty. To know a thing, we must look at it. How can we look at the sun? It is so very bright that our eyes are dazzled in gazing upon it. We have to turn away, or they would be put out,—the sight, I mean. It is true, we might use smoked glass, but that is apt to come off on the nose. How, then, if we cannot look at it, can we find out about it? The noonday would seem to be the better hour, when it is the sunniest; but, besides injuring the eyes, it is painful to the neck to look up for a long time. It is easy to say that our examination of this heavenly body should take place at sunrise, when we could look at it more on a level, without having to endanger the spine. But how many people are up at sunrise? Those who get up early do it because they are compelled to, and have something else to do than look at the sun.

The milkman goes forth to carry the daily milk, the ice-man to leave the daily ice. But either of these would be afraid of exposing their vehicles to the heating orb of day,—the milkman afraid of turning the milk, the ice-man timorous of melting his ice,—and they probably avoid those directions where they shall meet the sun's rays. The student, who might inform us, has been burning the midnight oil. The student is not in the mood to consider the early sun.

There remains to us the evening, also,—the leisure hour of the day. But, alas! our houses are not built with an adaptation to this subject. They are seldom made to look toward the sunset. A careful inquiry and close observation, such as have been called for in preparation of this paper, have developed the fact that not a single house in this town faces the sunset! There may be windows looking that way, but in such a case there is always a barn between. I can testify to this from personal observations, because, with my brothers, we have walked through the several streets of this town with notebooks, carefully noting every house looking upon the sunset, and have found none from which the sunset could be studied. Sometimes it was the next house, sometimes a row of houses, or its own wood-house, that stood in the way.

Of course, a study of the sun might be pursued out of doors. But in summer, sunstroke would be likely to follow; in winter, neuralgia and cold. And how could you consult your books, your dictionaries, your encyclopædias? There seems to be no hour of the day for studying the sun. You might go to the East to see it at its rising, or to the West to gaze upon its setting, but—you don't.

Here Elizabeth Eliza came to a pause. She had written five different endings, and had brought them all, thinking, when the moment came, she would choose one of them. She was pausing to select one, and inadvertently said, to close the phrase, "you don't." She had not meant to use the expression, which she would not have thought sufficiently imposing,—it dropped out unconsciously,—but it was received as a close with rapturous applause.

She had read slowly, and now that the audience applauded at such a length, she had time to feel she was much exhausted and glad of an end. Why not stop there, though there were some pages more? Applause, too, was heard from the outside. Some of the gentlemen had come,—Mr. Peterkin, Agamemnon, and Solomon John, with others,—and demanded admission.

"Since it is all over, let them in," said Ann Maria Bromwick.

Elizabeth Eliza assented, and rose to shake hands with her applauding friends.

II.

ELIZABETH ELIZA'S COMMONPLACE-BOOK.

I am going to jot down, from time to time, any suggestions that occur to me that will be of use in writing another paper, in case I am called upon. I might be asked unexpectedly for certain occasions, if anybody happened to be prevented from coming to a meeting.

I have not yet thought of a subject, but I think that is not of as much consequence as to gather the ideas. It seems as if the ideas might suggest the subject, even if the subject does not suggest the ideas.

Now, often a thought occurs to me in the midst, perhaps, of conversation with others; but I forget it afterwards, and spend a great deal of time in trying to think what it was I was thinking of, which might have been very valuable.

I have indeed, of late, been in the habit of writing such thoughts on scraps of paper, and have often left the table to record some idea that occurred to me; but, looking up the paper and getting ready to write it, the thought has escaped me.

Then again, when I have written it, it has been on the backs of envelopes or the off sheet of a note, and it has been lost, perhaps thrown into the scrap-basket. Amanda is a little careless about such things; and, indeed, I have before encouraged her in throwing away old envelopes, which do not seem of much use otherwise, so perhaps she is not to blame.

The more I think of it, the more does it seem to me there would be an advantage if everybody should have the same number to their houses,—of course not everybody, but everybody acquainted. It is so hard to remember all the numbers; the streets you are not so likely to forget. Friends might combine to have the same number. What made me think of it was that we do have the same number as the Easterlys. To be sure, we are out of town, and they are in Boston; but it makes it so convenient, when I go into town to see the Easterlys, to remember that their number is the same as ours.

Agamemnon has lost his new silk umbrella. Yet the case was marked with his name in full, and the street address and the town. Of course he left the case at home, going out in the rain. He might have carried it with the address in his pocket, yet this would not have helped after losing the umbrella. Why not have a pocket for the case in the umbrella?

In shaking the dust from a dress, walk slowly backwards. This prevents the dust from falling directly on the dress again.

On Carving Duck.—It is singular that I can never get so much off the breast as other people do.

Perhaps I have it set on wrong side up.

I wonder why they never have catalogues for libraries arranged from the last letter of the name instead of the first.

There is our Italian teacher whose name ends with a "j," which I should remember much easier than the first letter, being so odd.

I cannot understand why a man should want to marry his wife's deceased sister. If she is dead, indeed, how can he? And if he has a wife, how wrong! I am very glad there is a law against it.

It is well, in prosperity, to be brought up as though you were living in adversity; then, if you have to go back to adversity, it is all the same.

On the other hand, it might be as well, in adversity, to act as though you were living in prosperity; otherwise, you would seem to lose the prosperity either way.

Solomon John has invented a new extinguisher. It is to represent a Turk smoking a pipe, which is to be hollow, and lets the smoke out. A very pretty idea!

A bee came stumbling into my room this morning, as it has done every spring since we moved here,—perhaps not the same bee. I think there must have been a family bee-line across this place before ever a house was built here, and the bees are trying for it every year.

Perhaps we ought to cut a window opposite.

There's room enough in the world for me and thee; go thou and trouble some one else,—as the man said when he put the fly out of the window.

Ann Maria thinks it would be better to fix upon a subject first; but then she has never yet written a paper herself, so she does not realize that you have to have some thoughts before you can write them. She should think, she says, that I would write about something that I see. But of what use is it for me to write about what everybody is seeing, as long as they can see it as well as I

12

do?

The paper about emergencies read last week was one of the best I ever heard; but, of course, it would not be worth while for me to write the same, even if I knew enough.

My commonplace-book ought to show me what to do for common things; and then I can go to lectures, or read the "Rules of Emergencies" for the uncommon ones.

Because, as a family, I think we are more troubled about what to do on the common occasions than on the unusual ones. Perhaps because the unusual things don't happen to us, or very seldom; and for the uncommon things, there is generally some one you can ask.

I suppose there really is not as much danger about these uncommon things as there is in the small things, because they don't happen so often, and because you are more afraid of them.

I never saw it counted up, but I conclude that more children tumble into mud-puddles than into the ocean or Niagara Falls, for instance. It was so, at least, with our little boys; but that may have been partly because they never saw the ocean till last summer, and have never been to Niagara. To be sure, they had seen the harbor from the top of Bunker Hill Monument, but there they could not fall in. They might have fallen off from the top of the monument, but did not. I am sure, for our little boys, they have never had the remarkable things happen to them. I suppose because they were so dangerous that they did not try them, like firing at marks and rowing boats. If they had used guns, they might have shot themselves or others; but guns have never been allowed in the house. My father thinks it is dangerous to have them. They might go off unexpected. They would require us to have gunpowder and shot in the house, which would be dangerous. Amanda, too, is a little careless. And we never shall forget the terrible time when the "fulminating paste" went off one Fourth of July. It showed what might happen even if you did not keep gunpowder in the house.

To be sure, Agamemnon and Solomon John are older now, and might learn the use of fire-arms; but even then they might shoot the wrong person—the policeman or some friends coming into the house—instead of the burglar.

And I have read of safe burglars going about. I don't know whether it means that it is safe for them or for us; I hope it is the latter. Perhaps it means that they go without fire-arms, making it safer for them.

I have the "Printed Rules for Emergencies," which will be of great use, as I should be apt to forget which to do for which. I mean I should be quite likely to do for burns and scalds what I ought to do for cramp. And when a person is choking, I might sponge from head to foot, which is what I ought to do to prevent a cold.

But I hope I shall not have a chance to practise. We have never had the case of a broken leg, and it would hardly be worth while to break one on purpose.

Then we have had no cases of taking poison, or bites from mad dogs, perhaps partly because we don't keep either poison or dogs; but then our neighbors might, and we ought to be prepared. We do keep cats, so that we do not need to have poison for the rats; and in this way we avoid both dangers,— from the dogs going mad, and from eating the poison by mistake instead of the rats.

To be sure, we don't quite get rid of the rats, and need a trap for the mice; but if you have a good family cat it is safer.

About window-curtains—I mean the drapery ones—we have the same trouble in deciding every year. We did not put any in the parlor windows when we moved, only window-shades, because there were so many things to be done, and we wanted time to make up our minds as to what we would have.

But that was years ago, and we have not decided yet, though we consider the subject every spring and fall.

The trouble is, if we should have heavy damask ones like the Bromwicks', it would be very dark in the winter, on account of the new, high building opposite.

Now, we like as much light as we can get in the winter, so we have always waited till summer, thinking we would have some light muslin ones, or else of the new laces. But in summer we like to have the room dark, and the sun does get round in the morning quite dazzling on the white shades. (We might have dark-colored shades, but there would be the same trouble of its being too dark in the winter.)

We seem to need the heavy curtains in summer and the light curtains in winter, which would look odd. Besides, in winter we do need the heavy curtains to shut out the draughts, while in summer we like all the air we can get.

I have been looking for a material that shall shut out the air and yet let in the light, or else shut out the light and let in the air; or else let in the light when you want it, and not when you don't. I have not found it yet; but there are so many new inventions that I dare say I shall come across it in time. They seem to have invented everything except a steamer that won't go up and down as well as across.

I never could understand about averages. I can't think why people are so fond of taking them,—men generally. It seems to me they tell anything but the truth. They try to tell what happens every evening, and they don't tell one evening right.

There was our Free Evening Cooking-school. We had a class of fourteen girls; and they admired it, and liked nothing better, and attended regularly. But Ann Maria made out the report according to the average of attendance on the whole number of nights in the ten weeks of the school, one evening a week; so she gave the numbers 12-3/5 each night.

Now the fact was, they all came every night except one, when there was such a storm, nobody went,—not even the teacher, nor Ann Maria, nor any of us. It snowed and it hailed and the wind blew, and our steps were so slippery Amanda could not go out to put on ashes; ice even on the upper steps. The janitor, who makes the fire, set out to go; but she was blown across the street, into the gutter. She did succeed in getting in to Ann Maria's, who said it was foolish to attempt it, and that nobody would go; and I am not sure but she spent the night there,—at Ann Maria's, I mean. Still, Ann Maria had to make up the account of the number of evenings of the whole course.

But it looks, in the report, as though there were never the whole fourteen there, and as though 1-2/5 of a girl stayed away every night, when the facts are we did not have a single absence, and the whole fourteen were there every night, except the night there was no school; and I have been told they all had on their things to come that night, but their mothers would not let them,— those that had mothers,—and they would have been blown away if they had come.

It seems to me the report does not present the case right, on account of the averages.

I think it is indeed the common things that trouble one to decide about, as I have said, since for the remarkable ones one can have advice. The way we do on such occasions is to ask our friends, especially the lady from Philadelphia.

Whatever we should have done without her, I am sure I cannot tell, for her advice is always inestimable. To be sure, she is not always here; but there is the daily mail (twice from here to Boston), and the telegraph, and to some places the telephone.

But for some common things there is not time for even the telephone.

Yesterday morning, for instance, going into Boston in the early train, I took the right side for a seat, as is natural, though I noticed that most of the passengers were crowding into the seats on the other side. I found, as we left the station, that I was on the sunny side, which was very uncomfortable. So I made up my mind to change sides, coming out. But, unexpectedly, I stayed in till afternoon at Mrs. Easterly's. It seems she had sent a note to ask me (which I found at night all right, when I got home), as Mr. Easterly was away. So I did not go out till afternoon. I did remember my determination to change sides in going out, and as I took the right going in, not to take the right going out. But then I remembered, as it was afternoon, the sun would have changed; so if the right side was wrong in the morning, it would be right in the afternoon. At any rate, it would be safe to take the other side. I did observe that most of the people took the opposite side, the left side; but I supposed they had not stopped to calculate.

When we came out of the station and from under the bridges, I found I was sitting in the sun again, the same way as in the morning, in spite of all my reasoning. Ann Maria, who had come late and taken the last seat on the other side, turned round and called across to me, "Why do you always take the sunny side? Do you prefer it?" I was sorry not to explain it to her, but she was too far off.

It might be safe to do what most of the other people do, when you cannot stop to inquire; but you cannot always tell, since very likely they may be mistaken. And then if they have taken all the seats, there is not room left for you. Still, this time, in coming out, I had reached the train in plenty of season, and might have picked out my seat, but then there was nobody there to show where most of the people would go. I might have changed when I saw where most would go; but I hate changing, and the best seats were all taken.

My father thinks it would be a good plan for Amanda to go to the Lectures on Physics. She has lived with us a great many years, and she still breaks as many things as she did at the beginning.

Dr. Murtrie, who was here the other night, said he learned when quite a boy, from some book on Physics, that if he placed some cold water in the bottom of a pitcher, before pouring in boiling-hot water, it would not break. Also, that in washing a glass or china pitcher in very hot water, the outside and inside should be in the hot water, or, as he said, should feel the hot water at the same time. I don't quite understand exactly how, unless the pitcher has a large mouth, when it might be put in sideways.

He told the reasons, which, being scientific, I cannot remember or understand.

If Amanda had known about this, she might have saved a great deal of valuable glass and china. Though it has not always been from hot water, the breaking, for I often think she has not the water hot enough; but often from a whole tray-full sliding out of her hand, as she was coming up-stairs, and everything on it broke.

But Dr. Murtrie said if she had learned more of the Laws of Physics she would not probably so often tip over the waiter.

The trouble is, however, remembering at the right time. She might have known the law perfectly well, and forgotten it just on the moment, or her dress coming in the way may have prevented.

Still, I should like very well myself to go to the Lectures on Physics. Perhaps I could find out something about scissors,—why it is they do always tumble down, and usually, though so heavy, without any noise, so that you do not know that they have fallen. I should say they had no law, because sometimes they are far under the sofa in one direction, or hidden behind the leg of the table in another, or perhaps not even on the floor, but buried in the groove at the back of the easy-chair, and you never find them till you have the chair covered again. I do feel always in the back of the chair now; but Amanda found mine, yesterday, in the groove of the sofa.

It is possible Elizabeth Eliza may have taken the remaining sheets of her commonplace-book abroad with her. We have not been able to recover them.

III.

THE PETERKINS PRACTISE TRAVELLING.

Long ago Mrs. Peterkin had been afraid of the Mohammedans, and would have dreaded to travel among them; but since the little boys had taken lessons of the Turk, and she had become familiar with his costume and method of sitting, she had felt less fear of them as a nation.

To be sure, the Turk had given but few lessons, as, soon after making his engagement, he had been obliged to go to New York to join a tobacconist's firm. Mr. Peterkin had not regretted his payment for instruction in advance; for the Turk had been very urbane in his manners, and had always assented to whatever the little boys or any of the family had said to him.

Mrs. Peterkin had expressed a desire to see the famous Cleopatra's Needle which had been brought from Egypt. She had heard it was something gigantic for a needle, and it would be worth a journey to New York. She wondered at their bringing it such a distance, and would have supposed that some of Cleopatra's family would have objected to it if they were living now.

Agamemnon said that was the truth; there was no one left to object; they were all mummies under ground, with such heavy pyramids over them that they would not easily rise to object.

Mr. Peterkin feared that all the pyramids would be brought away in time. Agamemnon said there were a great many remaining in Egypt. Still, he thought it would be well to visit Egypt soon, before they were all brought away, and nothing but the sand left. Mrs. Peterkin said she would be almost as willing to travel to Egypt as to New York, and it would seem more worth while to go so far to see a great many than to go to New York only for one needle.

"That would certainly be a needless expense," suggested Solomon John.

Elizabeth Eliza was anxious to see the Sphinx. Perhaps it would answer some of the family questions that troubled them day after day.

Agamemnon felt it would be a great thing for the education of the little boys. If they could have begun with the Egyptian hieroglyphics before they had learned their alphabet, they would have begun at the right end. Perhaps it was not too late now to take them to Egypt, and let them begin upon its old learning. The little boys declared it was none too late. They could not say the alphabet backward now, and could never remember whether u came before v;

and the voyage would be a long one, and before they reached Egypt, very likely they would have forgotten all.

It was about this voyage that Mrs. Peterkin had much doubt. What she was afraid of was getting in and out of the ships and boats. She was afraid of tumbling into the water between, when she left the wharf. Elizabeth Eliza agreed with her mother in this, and began to calculate how many times they would have to change between Boston and Egypt.

There was the ferry-boat across to East Boston would make two changes; one more to get on board the steamer; then Liverpool—no, to land at Queenstown would make two more,—four, five changes; Liverpool, six. Solomon John brought the map, and they counted up. Dover, seven; Calais, eight; Marseilles, nine; Malta, if they landed, ten, eleven; and Alexandria, twelve changes.

Mrs. Peterkin shuddered at the possibilities, not merely for herself, but for the family. She could fall in but once, but by the time they should reach Egypt, how many would be left out of a family of eight? Agamemnon began to count up the contingencies. Eight times twelve would make ninety-six chances ($8 \times 12 = 96$). Mrs. Peterkin felt as if all might be swept off before the end could be reached.

Solomon John said it was not usual to allow more than one chance in a hundred. People always said "one in a hundred," as though that were the usual thing expected. It was not at all likely that the whole family would be swept off.

Mrs. Peterkin was sure they would not want to lose one; they could hardly pick out which they could spare, she felt certain. Agamemnon declared there was no necessity for such risks. They might go directly by some vessel from Boston to Egypt.

Solomon John thought they might give up Egypt, and content themselves with Rome. "All roads lead to Rome;" so it would not be difficult to find their way.

But Mrs. Peterkin was afraid to go. She had heard you must do as the Romans did if you went to Rome; and there were some things she certainly should not like to do that they did. There was that brute who killed Cæsar! And she should not object to the long voyage. It would give them time to think it all over.

Mr. Peterkin thought they ought to have more practice in travelling, to accustom themselves to emergencies. It would be fatal to start on so long a voyage and to find they were not prepared. Why not make their proposed excursion to the cousins at Gooseberry Beach, which they had been planning all summer? There they could practise getting in and out of a boat, and accustom themselves to the air of the sea. To be sure, the cousins were just moving up from the seashore, but they could take down a basket of luncheon, in order to give no trouble, and they need not go into the house.

Elizabeth Eliza had learned by heart, early in the summer, the list of trains, as she was sure they would lose the slip their cousins had sent them; and you never could find the paper that had the trains in when you wanted it. They must take the 7 A.M. train into Boston in time to go across to the station for the Gooseberry train at 7.45, and they would have to return from Gooseberry Beach by a 3.30 train. The cousins would order the "barge" to meet them on their arrival, and to come for them at 3 P.M., in time for the return train, if they were informed the day before. Elizabeth Eliza wrote them a postal card, giving them the information that they would take the early train. The "barge" was the name of the omnibus that took passengers to and from the Gooseberry station. Mrs. Peterkin felt that its very name was propitious to this Egyptian undertaking.

The day proved a fine one. On reaching Boston, Mrs. Peterkin and Elizabeth Eliza were put into a carriage with the luncheon-basket to drive directly to the station. Elizabeth Eliza was able to check the basket at the baggage-station, and to buy their "go-and-return" tickets before the arrival of the rest of the party, which appeared, however, some minutes before a quarter of eight. Mrs. Peterkin counted the little boys. All were there. This promised well for Egypt. But their joy was of short duration. On presenting their tickets at the gate of entrance, they were stopped. The Gooseberry train had gone at 7.35! The Mattapan train was now awaiting its passengers. Impossible! Elizabeth Eliza had repeated 7.45 every morning through the summer. It must be the Gooseberry train. But the conductor would not yield. If they wished to go to Mattapan they could go; if to Gooseberry, they must wait till the 5 P.M. train.

Mrs. Peterkin was in despair. Their return train was 3.30; how could 5 P.M. help them?

Mr. Peterkin, with instant decision, proposed they should try something else. Why should not they take their luncheon-basket across some ferry? This would give them practice. The family hastily agreed to this. What could be better? They went to the baggage-office, but found their basket had gone in the 7.35 train! They had arrived in time, and could have gone too. "If we had only been checked!" exclaimed Mrs. Peterkin. The baggage-master, showing a tender interest, suggested that there was a train for Plymouth at eight, which would take them within twelve miles of Gooseberry Beach, and they might find "a team" there to take them across. Solomon John and the little boys were delighted with the suggestion.

"We could see Plymouth Rock," said Agamemnon.

But hasty action would be necessary. Mr. Peterkin quickly procured tickets for Plymouth, and no official objected to their taking the 8 A.M. train. They were all safely in the train. This had been a test expedition; and each of the party had taken something, to see what would be the proportion of things lost to those remembered. Mr. Peterkin had two umbrellas, Agamemnon an atlas and spyglass, and the little boys were taking down two cats in a basket. All were safe.

"I am glad we have decided upon Plymouth," said Mr. Peterkin. "Before seeing the pyramids of Egypt we certainly ought to know something of Plymouth Rock. I should certainly be quite ashamed, when looking at their great obelisks, to confess that I had never seen our own Rock."

The conductor was attracted by this interesting party. When Mr. Peterkin told him of their mistake of the morning, and that they were bound for Gooseberry Beach, he advised them to stop at Kingston, a station nearer the beach. They would have but four miles to drive, and a reduction could be effected on their tickets. The family demurred. Were they ready now to give up Plymouth? They would lose time in going there. Solomon John, too, suggested it would be better, chronologically, to visit Plymouth on their return from Egypt, after they had seen the earliest things.

This decided them to stop at Kingston.

But they found here no omnibus nor carriage to take them to Gooseberry. The station-master was eager to assist them, and went far and near in search of some sort of wagon. Hour after hour passed away, the little boys had shared their last peanut, and gloom was gathering over the family, when Solomon John came into the station to say there was a photographer's cart on the other side of the road. Would not this be a good chance to have their photographs taken for their friends before leaving for Egypt? The idea reanimated the whole party, and they made their way to the cart, and into it, as the door was open. There was, however, no photographer there.

Agamemnon tried to remember what he had read of photography. As all the materials were there, he might take the family's picture. There would indeed be a difficulty in introducing his own. Solomon John suggested they might arrange the family group, leaving a place for him. Then, when all was ready, he could put the curtain over the box, take his place hastily, then pull away the curtain by means of a string. And Solomon John began to look around for a string while the little boys felt in their pockets.

21

Agamemnon did not exactly see how they could get the curtain back. Mr. Peterkin thought this of little importance. They would all be glad to sit some time after travelling so long. And the longer they sat the better for the picture, and perhaps somebody would come along in time to put back the curtain. They began to arrange the group. Mr. and Mrs. Peterkin were placed in the middle, sitting down. Elizabeth Eliza stood behind them, and the little boys knelt in front with the basket of cats. Solomon John and Agamemnon were also to stand behind, Agamemnon leaning over his father's shoulder. Solomon John was still looking around for a string when the photographer himself appeared. He was much surprised to find a group all ready for him. He had gone off that morning for a short holiday, but was not unwilling to take the family, especially when he heard they were soon going to Egypt. He approved of the grouping made by the family, but suggested that their eyes should not all be fixed upon the same spot. Before the pictures were finished, the station-master came to announce that two carriages were found to take the party to Gooseberry Beach.

"There is no hurry," said Mr. Peterkin, "Let the pictures be finished; they have made us wait, we can keep them waiting as long as we please."

The result, indeed, was very satisfactory. The photographer pronounced it a remarkably fine group. Elizabeth Eliza's eyes were lifted to the heavens perhaps a little too high. It gave her a rapt expression not customary with her; but Mr. Peterkin thought she might look in that way in the presence of the Sphinx. It was necessary to have a number of copies, to satisfy all the friends left behind when they should go to Egypt; and it certainly would not be worth while to come again so great a distance for more.

It was therefore a late hour when they left Kingston. It took some time to arrange the party in two carriages. Mr. Peterkin ought to be in one, Mrs. Peterkin in the other; but it was difficult to divide the little boys, as all wished to take charge of the cats. The drive, too, proved longer than was expected,— six miles instead of four.

When they reached their cousin's door, the "barge" was already standing there.

"It has brought our luncheon-basket!" exclaimed Solomon John.

"I am glad of it," said Agamemnon, "for I feel hungry enough for it."

He pulled out his watch. It was three o'clock!

This was indeed the "barge," but it had come for their return. The Gooseberry cousins, much bewildered that the family did not arrive at the time expected, had forgotten to send to countermand it. And the "barge" driver, supposing the family had arrived by the other station, had taken occasion to bring up the lunch-basket, as it was addressed to the Gooseberry cousins. The cousins flocked out to meet them. "What had happened? What had delayed them? They were glad to see them at last."

Mrs. Peterkin, when she understood the state of the case, insisted upon getting directly into the "barge" to return, although the driver said there would be a few moments to spare. Some of the cousins busied themselves in opening the luncheon-basket, and a part led the little boys and Agamemnon and Solomon John down upon the beach in front of the house; there would be a few moments for a glance at the sea. Indeed, the little boys ventured in their India-rubber boots to wade in a little way, as the tide was low. And Agamemnon and Solomon John walked to look at a boat that was drawn up on the beach, and got into it and out of it for practice, till they were all summoned back to the house.

It was indeed time to go. The Gooseberry cousins had got out the luncheon, and had tried to persuade the family to spend the night. Mrs. Peterkin declared this would be impossible. They never had done such a thing. So they went off, eating their luncheon as they went, the little boys each with a sandwich in one hand and a piece of cake in the other.

Mrs. Peterkin was sure they should miss the train or lose some of the party. No, it was a great success; for all, and more than all, were found in the train: slung over the arm of one of the little boys was found the basket containing the cats. They were to have left the cats, but in their haste had brought them away again.

This discovery was made in a search for the tickets which Elizabeth Eliza had bought, early in the morning, to go and return; they were needed now for return. She was sure she had given them to her father. Mrs. Peterkin supposed that Mr. Peterkin must have changed them for the Kingston tickets. The little boys felt in their pockets, Agamemnon and Solomon John in theirs. In the excitement, Mrs. Peterkin insisted upon giving up her copy of their new photograph, and could not be satisfied till the conductor had punched it. At last the tickets were found in the outer lappet of Elizabeth Eliza's hand-bag. She had looked for them in the inner part.

It was after this that Mr. Peterkin ventured to pronounce the whole expedition a success. To be sure, they had not passed the day at the beach, and had scarcely seen their cousins; but their object had been to practise travelling, and surely they had been travelling all day. Elizabeth Eliza had seen the sea, or thought she had. She was not sure—she had been so busy explaining to the cousins and showing the photographs. Agamemnon was sorry she had not walked with them to the beach, and tried getting in and out of the boat. Elizabeth Eliza regretted this. Of course it was not the same as getting into a boat on the sea, where it would be wobbling more, but the step must have been higher from the sand. Solomon John said there was some difficulty. He had jumped in, but was obliged to take hold of the side in getting out.

The little boys were much encouraged by their wade into the tide. They had been a little frightened at first when the splash came, but the tide had been low. On the whole, Mr. Peterkin continued, things had gone well. Even the bringing back of the cats might be considered a good omen. Cats were worshipped in Egypt, and they ought not to have tried to part with them. He was glad they had brought the cats. They gave the little boys an interest in feeding them while they were waiting at the Kingston station.

Their adventures were not quite over, as the station was crowded when they reached Boston. A military company had arrived from the South and was received by a procession. A number of distinguished guests also were expected, and the Peterkins found it difficult to procure a carriage. They had determined to take a carriage, so that they might be sure to reach their own evening train in season.

At last Mr. Peterkin discovered one that was empty, standing at the end of a long line. There would be room for Mrs. Peterkin, Elizabeth Eliza, himself, and the little boys, and Agamemnon and Solomon John agreed to walk behind in order to keep the carriage in sight. But they were much disturbed when they found they were going at so slow a pace. Mr. Peterkin called to the coachman in vain. He soon found that they had fallen into the line of the procession, and the coachman was driving slowly on behind the other carriages. In vain Mr. Peterkin tried to attract the driver's attention. He put his head out of one window after another, but only to receive the cheers of the populace ranged along the sidewalk. He opened the window behind the coachman and pulled his coat. But the cheering was so loud that he could not make himself heard. He tried to motion to the coachman to turn down one of the side streets, but in answer the driver pointed out with his whip the crowds of people. Mr. Peterkin, indeed, saw it would be impossible to make their way through the throng that filled every side street which they crossed. Mrs. Peterkin looked out of the back window for Agamemnon and Solomon John. They were walking side by side, behind the carriage, taking off their hats, and bowing to the people cheering on either side.

"They are at the head of a long row of men, walking two by two," said Mrs. Peterkin.

"They are part of the procession," said Elizabeth Eliza.

"We are part of the procession," Mr. Peterkin answered.

"I rather like it," said Mrs. Peterkin, with a calm smile, as she looked out of the window and bowed in answer to a cheer.

"Where do you suppose we shall go?" asked Elizabeth Eliza.

"I have often wondered what became of a procession," said Mr. Peterkin. "They are always going somewhere, but I never could tell where they went to."

"We shall find out!" exclaimed the little boys, who were filled with delight, looking now out of one window, now out of the other.

"Perhaps we shall go to the armory," said one.

This alarmed Mrs. Peterkin. Sounds of martial music were now heard, and the noise of the crowd grew louder. "I think you ought to ask where we are going," she said to Mr. Peterkin.

"It is not for us to decide," he answered calmly. "They have taken us into the procession. I suppose they will show us the principal streets, and will then leave us at our station."

This, indeed, seemed to be the plan. For two hours more the Peterkins, in their carriage, and Agamemnon and Solomon John, afoot, followed on. Mrs. Peterkin looked out upon rows and rows of cheering people. The little boys waved their caps.

"It begins to be a little monotonous," said Mrs. Peterkin, at last.

"I am afraid we have missed all the trains," said Elizabeth Eliza, gloomily. But Mr. Peterkin's faith held to the last, and was rewarded. The carriage reached the square in which stood the railroad station. Mr. Peterkin again seized the lapels of the coachman's coat and pointed to the station, and he was able to turn his horses in that direction. As they left the crowd, they received a parting cheer. It was with difficulty that Agamemnon and Solomon John broke from the ranks.

"That was a magnificent reception!" exclaimed Mr. Peterkin, wiping his brow, after paying the coachman twice his fee. But Elizabeth Eliza said,—

"But we have lost all the trains, I am sure."

They had lost all but one. It was the last.

"And we have lost the cats!" the little boys suddenly exclaimed. But Mrs. Peterkin would not allow them to turn back in search of them.

IV.

THE PETERKINS' EXCURSION FOR MAPLE SUGAR.

It was, to be sure, a change of plan to determine to go to Grandfather's for a maple-sugaring instead of going to Egypt! But it seemed best. Egypt was not given up,—only postponed. "It has lasted so many centuries," sighed Mr. Peterkin, "that I suppose it will not crumble much in one summer more."

The Peterkins had determined to start for Egypt in June, and Elizabeth Eliza had engaged her dressmaker for January; but after all their plans were made, they were told that June was the worst month of all to go to Egypt in,— that they would arrive in midsummer, and find the climate altogether too hot, —that people who were not used to it died of it. Nobody thought of going to Egypt in summer; on the contrary, everybody came away. And what was worse, Agamemnon learned that not only the summers were unbearably hot, but there really was no Egypt in summer,—nothing to speak of,—nothing but water; for there was a great inundation of the river Nile every summer, which completely covered the country, and it would be difficult to get about except in boats.

Mr. Peterkin remembered he had heard something of the sort, but he did not suppose it had been kept up with the modern improvements.

Mrs. Peterkin felt that the thing must be very much exaggerated. She could not believe the whole country would be covered, or that everybody would leave; as summer was surely the usual time for travel, there must be strangers there, even if the natives left. She would not be sorry if there were fewer of the savages. As for the boats, she supposed after their long voyage they would all be used to going about in boats; and she had thought seriously of practising, by getting in and out of the rocking-chair from the sofa.

The family, however, wrote to the lady from Philadelphia, who had travelled in Egypt, and whose husband knew everything about Egypt that could be known,—that is, everything that had already been dug up, though he could only guess at what might be brought to light next.

The result was a very earnest recommendation not to leave for Egypt till the autumn. Travellers did not usually reach there before December, though October might be pleasant on account of the fresh dates.

So the Egypt plan was reluctantly postponed; and, to make amends for the disappointment to the little boys, an excursion for maple syrup was proposed instead.

Mr. Peterkin considered it almost a necessity. They ought to acquaint themselves with the manufactures of their own new country before studying those of the oldest in the world. He had been inquiring into the products of Egypt at the present time, and had found sugar to be one of their staples. They ought, then, to understand the American methods and compare them with those of Egypt. It would be a pretty attention, indeed, to carry some of the maple sugar to the principal dignitaries of Egypt.

But the difficulties in arranging an excursion proved almost as great as for going to Egypt. Sugar-making could not come off until it was warm enough for the sun to set the sap stirring. On the other hand, it must be cold enough for snow, as you could only reach the woods on snow-sleds. Now, if there were sun enough for the sap to rise, it would melt the snow; and if it were cold enough for sledding, it must be too cold for the syrup. There seemed an impossibility about the whole thing. The little boys, however, said there always had been maple sugar every spring,—they had eaten it; why shouldn't there be this spring?

Elizabeth Eliza insisted gloomily that this was probably old sugar they had eaten,—you never could tell in the shops.

Mrs. Peterkin thought there must be fresh sugar occasionally, as the old would have been eaten up. She felt the same about chickens. She never could understand why there were only the old, tough ones in the market, when there were certainly fresh young broods to be seen around the farm-houses every year. She supposed the market-men had begun with the old, tough fowls, and so they had to go on so. She wished they had begun the other way; and she had done her best to have the family eat up the old fowls, hoping they might, some day, get down to the young ones.

As to the uncertainty about the weather, she suggested they should go to Grandfather's the day before. But how can you go the day before, when you don't yet know the day?

All were much delighted, therefore, when Hiram appeared with the wood-sled, one evening, to take them, as early as possible the next day, to their grandfather's. He reported that the sap had started, the kettles had been on some time, there had been a light snow for sleighing, and to-morrow promised to be a fine day. It was decided that he should take the little boys and Elizabeth Eliza early, in the wood-sled; the others would follow later, in the carry-all.

Mrs. Peterkin thought it would be safer to have some of the party go on wheels, in case of a general thaw the next day.

A brilliant sun awoke them in the morning. The wood-sled was filled with hay, to make it warm and comfortable, and an arm-chair was tied in for Elizabeth Eliza. But she was obliged to go first to visit the secretary of the Circumambient Society, to explain that she should not be present at their evening meeting. One of the rules of this society was to take always a winding road when going upon society business, as the word "circumambient" means "compassing about." It was one of its laws to copy Nature as far as possible, and a straight line is never seen in Nature. Therefore she could not send a direct note to say she should not be present; she could only hint it in general conversation with the secretary; and she was obliged to take a roundabout way to reach the secretary's house, where the little boys called for her in her wood-sled.

What was her surprise to find eight little boys instead of three! In passing the school-house they had picked up five of their friends, who had reached the school door a full hour before the time. Elizabeth Eliza thought they ought to inquire if their parents would be willing they should go, as they all expected to spend the night at Grandfather's. Hiram thought it would require too much time to stop for the consent of ten parents; if the sun kept on at this rate, the snow would be gone before they should reach the woods. But the little boys said most of the little boys lived in a row, and Elizabeth Eliza felt she ought not to take the boys away for all night without their parents' knowledge. The consent of two mothers and two fathers was gained, and Mr. Dobson was met in the street, who said he would tell the other mother. But at each place they were obliged to stop for additional tippets and great-coats and India-rubber boots for the little boys. At the Harrimans', too, the Harriman girls insisted on dressing up the wood-sled with evergreens, and made one of the boys bring their last Christmas-tree, that was leaning up against the barn, to set it up in the back of the sled, over Elizabeth Eliza. All this made considerable delay; and when they reached the high-road again, the snow was indeed fast melting. Elizabeth Eliza was inclined to turn back, but Hiram said they would find the sleighing better farther up among the hills. The armchair joggled about a good deal, and the Christmas-tree creaked behind her; and Hiram was obliged to stop occasionally and tie in the chair and the tree more firmly.

But the warm sun was very pleasant, the eight little boys were very lively, and the sleigh-bells jingled gayly as they went on.

It was so late when they reached the wood-road that Hiram decided they had better not go up the hill to their grandfather's, but turn off into the woods.

"Your grandfather will be there by this time," he declared.

Elizabeth Eliza was afraid the carry-all would miss them, and thought they had better wait. Hiram did not like to wait longer, and proposed that one or two of the little boys should stop to show the way. But it was so difficult to decide which little boys should stay that he gave it up. Even to draw lots would take time. So he explained that there was a lunch hidden somewhere in the straw; and the little boys thought it an admirable time to look it up, and it was decided to stop in the sun at the corner of the road. Elizabeth Eliza felt a little jounced in the armchair, and was glad of a rest; and the little boys soon discovered an ample lunch,—just what might have been expected from Grandfather's,—apple-pie and doughnuts, and plenty of them! "Lucky we brought so many little boys!" they exclaimed.

Hiram, however, began to grow impatient. "There 'll be no snow left," he exclaimed, "and no afternoon for the syrup!"

But far in the distance the Peterkin carry-all was seen slowly approaching through the snow, Solomon John waving a red handkerchief. The little boys waved back, and Hiram ventured to enter upon the wood-road, but at a slow pace, as Elizabeth Eliza still feared that by some accident the family might miss them.

It was with difficulty that the carry-all followed in the deep but soft snow, in among the trunks of the trees and over piles of leaves hidden in the snow. They reached at last the edge of a meadow; and on the high bank above it stood a row of maples, a little shanty by the side, a slow smoke proceeding from its chimney. The little boys screamed with delight, but there was no reply. Nobody there!

"The folks all gone!" exclaimed Hiram; "then we must be late." And he proceeded to pull out a large silver watch from a side pocket. It was so large that he seldom was at the pains to pull it out, as it took time; but when he had succeeded at last, and looked at it, he started.

"Late, indeed! It is four o'clock, and we were to have been here by eleven; they have given you up."

The little boys wanted to force in the door; but Hiram said it was no use,— they wouldn't understand what to do, and he should have to see to the horses, —and it was too late, and it was likely they had carried off all the syrup. But he thought a minute, as they all stood in silence and gloom; and then he guessed they might find some sugar at Deacon Spear's, close by, on the back road, and that would be better than nothing. Mrs. Peterkin was pretty cold, and glad not to wait in the darkening wood; so the eight little boys walked through the wood-path, Hiram leading the way; and slowly the carry-all followed.

They reached Deacon Spear's at length; but only Mrs. Spear was at home. She was very deaf, but could explain that the family had taken all their syrup

29

to the annual festival.

"We might go to the festival," exclaimed the little boys.

"It would be very well," said Mrs. Peterkin, "to eat our fresh syrup there."

But Mrs. Spear could not tell where the festival was to be, as she had not heard; perhaps they might know at Squire Ramsay's. Squire Ramsay's was on their way to Grandfather's, so they stopped there; but they learned that the "Squire's folks had all gone with their syrup to the festival," but the man who was chopping wood did not know where the festival was to be.

"They 'll know at your grandfather's," said Mrs. Peterkin, from the carry-all.

"Yes, go on to your grandfather's," advised Mr. Peterkin, "for I think I felt a drop of rain." So they made the best of their way to Grandfather's.

At the moment they reached the door of the house, a party of young people whom Elizabeth Eliza knew came by in sleighs. She had met them all when visiting at her grandfather's.

"Come along with us," they shouted; "we are all going down to the sugar festival."

"That is what we have come for," said Mr. Peterkin.

"Where is it?" asked Solomon John.

"It is down your way," was the reply.

"It is in your own New Hall," said another. "We have sent down all our syrup. The Spears and Ramsays and Doolittles have gone on with theirs. No time to stop; there's good sleighing on the old road."

There was a little consultation with the grandfather. Hiram said that he could take them back with the wood-sled, when he heard there was sleighing on the old road; and it was decided that the whole party should go in the wood-sled, with the exception of Mr. Peterkin, who would follow on with the carry-all. Mrs. Peterkin would take the arm-chair, and cushions were put in for Elizabeth Eliza, and more apple-pie for all. No more drops of rain appeared, though the clouds were thickening over the setting sun.

"All the way back again," sighed Mrs. Peterkin, "when we might have stayed at home all day, and gone quietly out to the New Hall!" But the little boys thought the sledding all day was great fun,—and the apple-pie! "And we did see the kettle through the cracks of the shanty!"

"It is odd the festival should be held at the New Hall," said Elizabeth Eliza; "for the secretary did say something about the society meeting there to-night, being so far from the centre of the town."

This hall was so called because it was once a new hall, built to be used for lectures, assemblies, and entertainments of this sort, for the convenience of the inhabitants who had collected about some flourishing factories.

"You can go to your own Circumambient Society, then!" exclaimed Solomon John.

"And in a truly circumambient manner," said Agamemnon; and he explained to the little boys that they could now understand the full meaning of the word, for surely Elizabeth Eliza had taken the most circumambient way of reaching the place by coming away from it.

"We little thought, when we passed it early this morning," said Elizabeth Eliza, "that we should come back to it for our maple sugar."

"It is odd the secretary did not tell you they were going to join the sugar festival," said Mrs. Peterkin.

"It is one of the rules of the society," said Elizabeth Eliza, "that the secretary never tells anything directly. She only hinted at the plan of the New Hall."

"I don't see how you can find enough to talk about," said Solomon John.

"We can tell of things that never have happened," said Elizabeth Eliza, "or that are not likely to happen, and wonder what would have happened if they had happened."

They arrived at the festival at last, but very late, and glad to find a place that was warm. There was a stove at each end of the hall, and an encouraging sound and smell from the simmering syrup. There were long tables down the hall, on which were placed, in a row, first a bowl of snow, then a pile of saucers and spoons, then a plate of pickles, intended to whet the appetite for more syrup; another of bread, then another bowl of snow, and so on. Hot syrup was to be poured on the snow and eaten as candy.

The Peterkin family were received at this late hour with a wild enthusiasm. Elizabeth Eliza was an especial heroine, and was made directly the president of the evening. Everybody said that she had best earned the distinction; for had she not come to the meeting by the longest way possible, by going away from it? The secretary declared that the principles of the society had been completely carried out. She had always believed that if left to itself, information would spread itself in a natural instead of a forced way.

"Now, in this case, if I had written twenty-nine notifications to this meeting, I should have wasted just so much of my time. But the information has disseminated naturally. Ann Maria said what a good plan it would be to have the Circumambients go to the sugaring at the New Hall. Everybody said it would be a good plan. Elizabeth Eliza came and spoke of the sugaring, and I spoke of the New Hall."

"But if you had told Elizabeth Eliza that all the maple syrup was to be brought here—" began Mrs. Peterkin.

"We should have lost our excursion for maple syrup," said Mr. Peterkin.

Later, as they reached home in the carry-all (Hiram having gone back with the wood-sled), Mr. and Mrs. Peterkin, after leaving little boys at their homes all along the route, found none of their own to get out at their own door. They must have joined Elizabeth Eliza, Agamemnon, and Solomon John in taking a circuitous route home with the rest of the Circumambients.

"The little boys will not be at home till midnight," said Mrs. Peterkin, anxiously. "I do think this is carrying the thing too far, after such a day!"

"Elizabeth Eliza will feel that she has acted up to the principles of the society," said Mr. Peterkin, "and we have done our best; for, as the little boys said, 'we did see the kettle.'"

V.

THE PETERKINS "AT HOME."

Might not something be done by way of farewell before leaving for Egypt? They did not want to give another tea-party, and could not get in all at dinner. They had had charades and a picnic. Elizabeth Eliza wished for something unusual, that should be remembered after they had left for Egypt. Why should it not be a fancy ball? There never had been one in the place.

Mrs. Peterkin hesitated. Perhaps for that reason they ought not to attempt it. She liked to have things that other people had. She however objected most to the "ball" part. She could indeed still dance a minuet, but she was not sure she could get on in the "Boston dip."

The little boys said they would like the "fancy" part and "dressing up." They remembered their delight when they browned their faces for Hindus, at their charades, just for a few minutes; and what fun it would be to wear their costumes through a whole evening! Mrs. Peterkin shook her head; it was days and days before the brown had washed out of their complexions.

Still, she too was interested in the "dressing up." If they should wear costumes, they could make them of things that might be left behind, that they had done wearing, if they could only think of the right kind of things.

Mrs. Peterkin, indeed, had already packed up, although they were not to leave for two months, for she did not want to be hurried at the last. She and Elizabeth Eliza went on different principles in packing.

Elizabeth Eliza had been told that you really needed very little to travel with,—merely your travelling dress and a black silk. Mrs. Peterkin, on the contrary, had heard it was best to take everything you had, and then you need not spend your time shopping in Paris. So they had decided upon adopting both ways. Mrs. Peterkin was to take her "everything," and already had all the shoes and stockings she should need for a year or two. Elizabeth Eliza, on the other hand, prepared a small valise. She consoled herself with the thought that if she should meet anything that would not go into it, she could put it in one of her mother's trunks.

It was resolved to give the fancy ball.

Mr. Peterkin early determined upon a character. He decided to be Julius Cæsar. He had a bald place on the top of his head, which he was told resembled that of the great Roman; and he concluded that the dress would be a simple one to get up, requiring only a sheet for a toga.

Agamemnon was inclined to take the part which his own name represented, and he looked up the costume of the Greek king of men. But he was dissatisfied with the representation given of him in Dr. Schliemann's "Mykenæ." There was a picture of Agamemnon's mask, but very much battered. He might get a mask made in that pattern, indeed, and the little boys were delighted with the idea of battering it. Agamemnon would like to wear a mask, then he would have no trouble in keeping up his expression. But Elizabeth Eliza objected to the picture in Dr. Schliemann's book; she did not like it for Agamemnon,—it was too slanting in the eyes. So it was decided he should take the part of Nick Bottom, in "Midsummer Night's Dream." He could then wear the ass's head, which would have the same advantage as a mask, and would conceal his own face entirely. Then he could be making up any face he pleased in the ass's head, and would look like an ass without any difficulty, while his feet would show he was not one. Solomon John thought that they might make an ass's head if they could get a pattern, or could see the real animal and form an idea of the shape. Barnum's Circus would be along in a few weeks, and they could go on purpose to study the donkeys, as there usually was more than one donkey in the circus. Agamemnon, however, in going with a friend to a costumer's in Boston, found an ass's head already made.

The little boys found in an illustrated paper an accurate description of the Hindu snake-charmer's costume, and were so successful in their practice of shades of brown for the complexion, that Solomon John decided to take the part of Othello, and use some of their staining fluid.

There was some discussion as to consulting the lady from Philadelphia, who was in town.

Solomon John thought they ought to practise getting on by themselves, for soon the Atlantic would lie between her and them. Mrs. Peterkin thought they could telegraph. Elizabeth Eliza wanted to submit to her two or three questions about the supper, and whether, if her mother were Queen Elizabeth, they could have Chinese lanterns. Was China invented at that time? Agamemnon was sure China was one of the oldest countries in the world and did exist, though perhaps Queen Elizabeth did not know it.

Elizabeth Eliza was relieved to find that the lady from Philadelphia thought the question not important. It would be impossible to have everything in the house to correspond with all the different characters, unless they selected some period to represent, such as the age of Queen Elizabeth. Of course, Elizabeth Eliza would not wish to do this when her father was to be Julius Cæsar.

The lady from Philadelphia advised Mrs. Peterkin to send for Jones the "caterer" to take charge of the supper. But his first question staggered her. How many did she expect?

They had not the slightest idea. They had sent invitations to everybody. The little boys proposed getting the directory of the place, and marking out the people they didn't know and counting up the rest. But even if this would give the number of invitations, it would not show how many would accept; and then there was no such directory. They could not expect answers, as their invitations were cards with "At Home" on them. One answer had come from a lady, that she too would be "at home" with rheumatism. So they only knew there was one person who would not come. Elizabeth Eliza had sent in Circumambient ways to all the members of that society,—by the little boys, for instance, who were sure to stop at the base-ball grounds, or somewhere, so a note was always delayed by them. One Circumambient note she sent by mail, purposely omitting the "Mass.," so that it went to the Dead-Letter Office, and came back six weeks after the party.

But the Peterkin family were not alone in commotion. The whole town was in excitement, for "everybody" had been invited. Ann Maria Bromwick had a book of costumes that she lent to a few friends, and everybody borrowed dresses or lent them, or went into town to the costumer's. Weeks passed in preparation. "What are you going to wear?" was the only question exchanged; and nobody answered, as nobody would tell.

At length the evening came,—a beautiful night in late summer, warm enough to have had the party out-of-doors; but the whole house was lighted up and thrown open, and Chinese lanterns hung in the portico and on the pillars of the piazzas.

At an early hour the Peterkins were arrayed in their costumes. The little boys had their legs and arms and faces browned early in the day, and wore dazzlingly white full trousers and white turbans.

Elizabeth Eliza had prepared a dress as Queen Elizabeth; but Solomon John was desirous that she should be Desdemona, and she gave up her costume to her mother. Mrs. Peterkin therefore wore a red wig which Ann Maria had found at a costumer's, a high ruff, and an old-fashioned brocade. She was not sure that it was proper for Queen Elizabeth to wear spectacles; but Queen Elizabeth must have been old enough, as she lived to be seventy. As for Elizabeth Eliza, in recalling the fact that Desdemona was smothered by pillows, she was so impressed by it that she decided she could wear the costume of a sheet-and-pillow-case party. So she wore a white figured silk that had been her mother's wedding-dress, and over it draped a sheet as a large mantle, and put a pillow-case upon her head, and could represent

Desdemona not quite smothered. But Solomon John wished to carry out the whole scene at the end.

As they stood together, all ready to receive, in the parlor at the appointed hour, Mr. Peterkin suddenly exclaimed,—

"This will never do! We are not the Peterkins,—we are distinguished guests! We cannot receive."

"We shall have to give up the party," said Mrs. Peterkin.

"Or our costumes," groaned Agamemnon from his ass's head.

"We must go out, and come in as guests," said Elizabeth Eliza, leading the way to a back door, for guests were already thronging in, and up the front stairs. They passed out by a piazza, through the hedge of hollyhocks, toward the front of the house. Through the side windows of the library they could see the company pouring in. The black attendant was showing them upstairs; some were coming down, in doubt whether to enter the parlors, as no one was there. The wide middle entrance hall was lighted brilliantly; so were the parlors on one side and the library on the other.

But nobody was there to receive! A flock of guests was assembling,— peasant girls, Italian, German, and Norman; Turks, Greeks, Persians, fish-wives, brigands, chocolate-women, Lady Washington, Penelope, Red Riding-hood, Joan of Arc, nuns, Amy Robsart, Leicester, two or three Mary Stuarts, Neapolitan fisher-boys, pirates of Penzance and elsewhere,—all lingering, some on the stairs, some going up, some coming down.

Charles I. without his head was entering the front door (a short gentleman, with a broad ruff drawn neatly together on top of his own head, which was concealed in his doublet below).

Three Hindu snake-charmers leaped wildly in and out among the throng, flinging about dark, crooked sticks for snakes.

There began to be a strange, deserted air about the house. Nobody knew what to do, where to go!

"Can anything have happened to the family?"

"Have they gone to Egypt?" whispered one.

No ushers came to show them in. A shudder ran through the whole assembly, the house seemed so uninhabited; and some of the guests were inclined to go away. The Peterkins saw it all through the long library-windows.

"What shall we do?" said Mr. Peterkin. "We have said *we* should be 'At

Home.'"

"And here we are, all out-of-doors among the hollyhocks," said Elizabeth Eliza.

"There are no Peterkins to 'receive,'" said Mr. Peterkin, gloomily.

"We might go in and change our costumes," said Mrs. Peterkin, who already found her Elizabethan ruff somewhat stiff; "but, alas! I could not get at my best dress."

"The company is filling all the upper rooms," said Elizabeth Eliza; "we cannot go back."

At this moment the little boys returned from the front door, and in a subdued whisper explained that the lady from Philadelphia was arriving.

"Oh, bring her here!" said Mrs. Peterkin. And Solomon John hastened to meet her.

She came, to find a strange group half lighted by the Chinese lanterns. Mr. Peterkin, in his white toga, with a green wreath upon his head, came forward to address her in a noble manner, while she was terrified by the appearance of Agamemnon's ass's head, half hidden among the leaves.

"What shall we do?" exclaimed Mr. Peterkin. "There are no Peterkins; yet we have sent cards to everybody that they are 'At Home'!"

The lady from Philadelphia, who had been allowed to come without costume, considered for a moment. She looked through the windows to the seething mass now crowding the entrance hall. The Hindu snake-charmers gambolled about her.

"*We* will receive as the Peterkin family!" she exclaimed. She inquired for a cap of Mrs. Peterkin's, with a purple satin bow, such as she had worn that very morning. Amanda was found by a Hindu, and sent for it and for a purple cross-over shawl that Mrs. Peterkin was wont to wear. The daughters of the lady from Philadelphia put on some hats of the little boys and their India-rubber boots. Hastily they went in through the back door and presented themselves, just as some of the wavering guests had decided to leave the house, it seeming so quiet and sepulchral.

The crowd now flocked into the parlors. The Peterkins themselves left the hollyhocks and joined the company that was entering; Mr. Peterkin, as Julius Cæsar, leading in Mrs. Peterkin, as Queen Elizabeth. Mrs. Peterkin hardly knew what to do, as she passed the parlor door; for one of the Osbornes, as Sir Walter Raleigh, flung a velvet cloak before her. She was uncertain whether she ought to step on it, especially as she discovered at that moment that she

37

had forgotten to take off her rubber overshoes, which she had put on to go through the garden. But as she stood hesitating, the lady from Philadelphia, as Mrs. Peterkin, beckoned her forward, and she walked over the ruby velvet as though it were a door-mat.

For another surprise stunned her,—there were three Mrs. Peterkins! Not only Mrs. Bromwick, but their opposite neighbor, had induced Amanda to take dresses of Mrs. Peterkin's from the top of the trunks, and had come in at the same moment with the lady from Philadelphia, ready to receive. She stood in the middle of the bow-window at the back of the room, the two others in the corners. Ann Maria Bromwick had the part of Elizabeth Eliza, and Agamemnon too was represented; and there were many sets of "little boys" in India-rubber boots, going in and out with the Hindu snake-charmers.

Mr. Peterkin had studied up his Latin grammar a little, in preparation for his part of Julius Cæsar. Agamemnon had reminded him that it was unnecessary, as Julius Cæsar in Shakspeare spoke in English. Still he now found himself using with wonderful ease Latin phrases such as "E pluribus unum," "lapsus linguæ," and "sine qua non," where they seemed to be appropriate.

Solomon John looked well as Othello, although by some he was mistaken for an older snake-charmer, with his brown complexion, glaring white trousers, and white shirt. He wore a white lawn turban that had belonged to his great-grandmother. His part, however, was more understood when he was with Elizabeth Eliza as Desdemona; for they occasionally formed a tableau, in which he pulled the pillow-case completely over her head.

Agamemnon was greeted with applause as Nick Bottom. He sang the song of the "ousel cock," but he could not make himself heard. At last he found a "Titania" who listened to him.

But none of the company attempted to carry out the parts represented by their costumes. Charles I. soon conversed with Oliver Cromwell and with the different Mary Stuarts, who chatted gayly, as though executions were every-day occurrences.

At first there was a little awkwardness. Nuns stood as quiet as if in their convent cells, and brave brigands hid themselves behind the doors; but as the different guests began to surprise each other, the sounds of laughter and talking increased. Every new-comer was led up to each several Mrs. Peterkin.

Then came a great surprise,—a band of music sounded from the piazza. Some of the neighbors had sent in the town band, as a farewell tribute. This added to the excitement of the occasion. Strains of dance-music were heard, and dancing was begun. Sir Walter Raleigh led out Penelope, and Red Riding-hood without fear took the arm of the fiercest brigand for a round dance.

The various groups wandered in and out. Elizabeth Eliza studied the costumes of her friends, and wished she had tried each one of them. The members of the Circumambient Society agreed that it would be always well to wear costumes at their meetings. As the principles of the society enforced a sort of uncertainty, if you always went in a different costume you would never have to keep up your own character. Elizabeth Eliza thought she should enjoy this. She had all her life been troubled with uncertainties and questions as to her own part of "Elizabeth Eliza," wondering always if she were doing the right thing. It did not seem to her that other people had such a bother. Perhaps they had simpler parts. They always seemed to know when to speak and when to be silent, while she was always puzzled as to what she should do as Elizabeth Eliza. Now, behind her pillow-case, she could look on and do nothing; all that was expected of her was to be smothered now and then. She breathed freely and enjoyed herself, because for the evening she could forget the difficult role of Elizabeth Eliza.

Mrs. Peterkin was bewildered. She thought it a good occasion to study how Mrs. Peterkin should act; but there were three Mrs. Peterkins. She found herself gazing first at one, then at another. Often she was herself called Mrs. Peterkin.

THE ASS'S HEAD PROVED HOT AND HEAVY, AND
AGAMEMNON WAS FORCED TO HANG IT OVER HIS ARM.

At supper-time the bewilderment increased. She was led in by the Earl of Leicester, as principal guest. Yet it was to her own dining-room, and she recognized her own forks and spoons among the borrowed ones, although the china was different (because their own set was not large enough to go round for so much company). It was all very confusing. The dance-music floated through the air. Three Mrs. Peterkins hovered before her, and two Agamemnons; for the ass's head proved hot and heavy, and Agamemnon was forced to hang it over his arm as he offered coffee to Titania. There seemed to be two Elizabeth Elizas, for Elizabeth Eliza had thrown back her pillow-case in order to eat her fruit-ice. Mr. Peterkin was wondering how Julius Cæsar would have managed to eat his salad with his fork, before forks were invented, and then he fell into a fit of abstraction, planning to say "Vale" to the guests as they left, but anxious that the word should not slip out before the time. Eight little boys and three Hindu snake-charmers were eating copiously of frozen pudding. Two Joans of Arc were talking to Charles I., who had found his head. All things seemed double to Mrs. Peterkin as they floated before her.

"Was she eating her own supper or somebody's else? Were they Peterkins, or were they not?"

Strains of dance-music sounded from the library. Yes, they were giving a fancy ball! The Peterkins were "At Home" for the last time before leaving for Egypt!

VI.

MRS. PETERKIN IN EGYPT.

The family had taken passage in the new line for Bordeaux. They supposed they had; but would they ever reach the vessel in New York? The last moments were terrific. In spite of all their careful arrangements, their planning and packing of the last year, it seemed, after all, as if everything were left for the very last day. There were presents for the family to be packed, six steamer-bags for Mrs. Peterkin, half a dozen satchels of salts-bottles for Elizabeth Eliza, Apollinaris water, lunch-baskets. All these must be disposed of.

On the very last day Elizabeth Eliza went into Boston to buy a bird, as she had been told she would be less likely to be sea-sick if she had a bird in a cage in her stateroom. Both she and her mother disliked the singing of caged birds, especially of canaries; but Mrs. Peterkin argued that they would be less likely to be homesick, as they never had birds at home. After long moments of indecision, Elizabeth Eliza determined upon two canary-birds, thinking she might let them fly as they approached the shore of Portugal, and they would then reach their native islands. This matter detained her till the latest train, so that on her return from Boston to their quiet suburban home, she found the whole family assembled in the station, ready to take the through express train to New York.

She did not have time, therefore, to go back to the house for her own things. It was now locked up and the key intrusted to the Bromwicks; and all the Bromwicks and the rest of the neighbors were at the station, ready to bid them good-by. The family had done their best to collect all her scattered bits of baggage; but all through her travels, afterward, she was continually missing something she had left behind, that she would have packed and had intended to bring.

They reached New York with half a day on their hands; and during this time Agamemnon fell in with some old college friends, who were going with a party to Greece to look up the new excavations. They were to leave the next day in a steamer for Gibraltar. Agamemnon felt that here was the place for him, and hastened to consult his family. Perhaps he could persuade them to change their plans and take passage with the party for Gibraltar. But he reached the pier just as the steamer for Bordeaux was leaving the shore. He was too late, and was left behind! Too late to consult them, too late even to join them! He examined his map, however,—one of his latest purchases, which he carried in his pocket,—and consoled himself with the fact that on reaching Gibraltar he could soon communicate with his family at Bordeaux, and he was easily reconciled to his fate.

It was not till the family landed at Bordeaux that they discovered the absence of Agamemnon. Every day there had been some of the family unable to come on deck,—sea-sick below. Mrs. Peterkin never left her berth, and constantly sent messages to the others to follow her example, as she was afraid some one of them would be lost overboard. Those who were on deck from time to time were always different ones, and the passage was remarkably quick; while, from the tossing of the ship, as they met rough weather, they were all too miserable to compare notes or count their numbers. Elizabeth Eliza especially had been exhausted by the voyage. She had not been many days seasick, but the incessant singing of the birds had deprived her of sleep. Then the necessity of talking French had been a great tax upon her. The other passengers were mostly French, and the rest of the family constantly appealed to her to interpret their wants, and explain them to the *garçon* once every day at dinner. She felt as if she never wished to speak another word in French; and the necessity of being interpreter at the hotel at Bordeaux, on their arrival, seemed almost too much for her. She had even forgotten to let her canary-birds fly when off shore in the Bay of Biscay, and they were still with her, singing incessantly, as if they were rejoicing over an approach to their native shores. She thought now she must keep them till their return, which they were already planning.

The little boys, indeed, would like to have gone back on the return trip of the steamer. A son of the steward told them that the return cargo consisted of dried fruits and raisins; that every stateroom, except those occupied with passengers, would be filled with boxes of raisins and jars of grapes; that these often broke open in the passage, giving a great opportunity for boys.

But the family held to their Egypt plan, and were cheered by making the acquaintance of an English party. At the *table d'hôte* Elizabeth Eliza by chance dropped her fork into her neighbor's lap. She apologized in French; her neighbor answered in the same language, which Elizabeth Eliza understood so well that she concluded she had at last met with a true Parisian, and ventured on more conversation, when suddenly they both found they were talking in English, and Elizabeth Eliza exclaimed, "I am so glad to meet an American," at the moment that her companion was saying, "Then you are an Englishwoman!"

From this moment Elizabeth Eliza was at ease, and indeed both parties were mutually pleased. Elizabeth Eliza's new friend was one of a large party, and she was delighted to find that they too were planning a winter in Egypt.

They were waiting till a friend should have completed her "cure" at Pau, and the Peterkins were glad also to wait for the appearance of Agamemnon, who might arrive in the next steamer.

One of the little boys was sure he had heard Agamemnon's voice the morning after they left New York, and was certain he must have been on board the vessel. Mr. Peterkin was not so sure. He now remembered that Agamemnon had not been at the dinner-table the very first evening; but then neither Mrs. Peterkin nor Solomon John was able to be present, as the vessel was tossing in a most uncomfortable manner, and nothing but dinner could have kept the little boys at table. Solomon John knew that Agamemnon had not been in his own stateroom during the passage, but he himself had seldom left it, and it had been always planned that Agamemnon should share that of a fellow-passenger.

However this might be, it would be best to leave Marseilles with the English party by the "P. & O." steamer. This was one of the English "Peninsular and Oriental" line, that left Marseilles for Alexandria, Egypt, and made a return trip directly to Southampton, England. Mr. Peterkin thought it might be advisable to take "go-and-return" tickets, coming back to Southampton; and Mrs. Peterkin liked the idea of no change of baggage, though she dreaded the longer voyage. Elizabeth Eliza approved of this return trip in the P. & O. steamer, and decided it would give a good opportunity to dispose of her canary-birds on her return.

The family therefore consoled themselves at Marseilles with the belief that Agamemnon would appear somehow. If not, Mr. Peterkin thought he could telegraph him from Marseilles, if he only knew where to telegraph to. But at Marseilles there was great confusion at the Hôtel de Noailles; for the English party met other friends, who persuaded them to take route together by Brindisi. Elizabeth Eliza was anxious to continue with her new English friend, and Solomon John was delighted with the idea of passing through the whole length of Italy. But the sight of the long journey, as she saw it on the map in the guide-book, terrified Mrs. Peterkin. And Mr. Peterkin had taken their tickets for the Marseilles line. Elizabeth Eliza still dwelt upon the charm of crossing under the Alps, while this very idea alarmed Mrs. Peterkin.

On the last morning the matter was still undecided. On leaving the hotel, it was necessary for the party to divide and take two omnibuses. Mr. and Mrs. Peterkin reached the steamer at the moment of departure, and suddenly Mrs. Peterkin found they were leaving the shore. As they crossed the broad gangway to reach the deck, she had not noticed they had left the pier; indeed, she had supposed that the steamer was one she saw out in the offing, and that they would be obliged to take a boat to reach it. She hurried from the group of travellers whom she had followed to find Mr. Peterkin reading from his guide-book to the little boys an explanation that they were passing the Château d'If, from which the celebrated historical character the Count of Monte Cristo had escaped by flinging himself into the sea.

"Where is Elizabeth Eliza? Where is Solomon John?" Mrs. Peterkin exclaimed, seizing Mr. Peterkin's arm. Where indeed? There was a pile of the hand-baggage of the family, but not that of Elizabeth Eliza, not even the bird-cage. "It was on the top of the other omnibus," exclaimed Mrs. Peterkin. Yes, one of the little boys had seen it on the pavement of the court-yard of the hotel, and had carried it to the omnibus in which Elizabeth Eliza was sitting. He had seen her through the window.

"Where is that other omnibus?" exclaimed Mrs. Peterkin, looking vaguely over the deck, as they were fast retreating from the shore. "Ask somebody what became of that other omnibus!" she exclaimed. "Perhaps they have gone with the English people," suggested Mr. Peterkin; but he went to the officers of the boat, and attempted to explain in French that one half of his family had been left behind. He was relieved to find that the officers could understand his French, though they did not talk English. They declared, however, it was utterly impossible to turn back. They were already two minutes and a half behind time on account of waiting for a party who had been very long in crossing the gangway.

Mr. Peterkin returned gloomily with the little boys to Mrs. Peterkin. "We cannot go back," he said, "we must content ourselves with going on; but I conclude we can telegraph from Malta. We can send a message to Elizabeth Eliza and Solomon John, telling them that they can take the next Marseilles P. & O. steamer in ten days, or that they can go back to Southampton for the next boat, which leaves at the end of this week. And Elizabeth Eliza may decide upon this," Mr. Peterkin concluded, "on account of passing so near the Canary Isles."

"She will be glad to be rid of the birds," said Mrs. Peterkin, calming herself.

These anxieties, however, were swallowed up in new trials. Mrs. Peterkin found that she must share her cabin (she found it was called "cabin," and not "stateroom," which bothered her and made her feel like Robinson Crusoe),— her cabin she must share with some strange ladies, while Mr. Peterkin and the little boys were carried to another part of the ship. Mrs. Peterkin remonstrated, delighted to find that her English was understood, though it was not listened to. It was explained to her that every family was divided in this way, and that she would meet Mr. Peterkin and the little boys at meal-times in the large *salon*—on which all the cabins opened—and on deck; and she was

45

obliged to content herself with this. Whenever they met their time was spent in concocting a form of telegram to send from Malta. It would be difficult to bring it into the required number of words, as it would be necessary to suggest three different plans to Elizabeth Eliza and Solomon John. Besides the two they had already discussed, there was to be considered the possibility of their having joined the English party. But Mrs. Peterkin was sure they must have gone back first to the Hôtel de Noailles, to which they could address their telegram.

She found, meanwhile, the ladies in her cabin very kind and agreeable. They were mothers returning to India, who had been home to England to leave their children, as they were afraid to expose them longer to the climate of India. Mrs. Peterkin could have sympathetic talks with them over their family photographs. Mrs. Peterkin's family-book was, alas! in Elizabeth Eliza's hand-bag. It contained the family photographs, from early childhood upward, and was a large volume, representing the children at every age.

At Malta, as he supposed, Mr. Peterkin and the little boys landed, in order to send their telegram. Indeed, all of the gentlemen among the passengers, and some of the ladies, gladly went on shore to visit the points of interest that could be seen in the time allotted. The steamer was to take in coal, and would not leave till early the next morning.

Mrs. Peterkin did not accompany them. She still had her fears about leaving the ship and returning to it, although it had been so quietly accomplished at Marseilles.

The party returned late at night, after Mrs. Peterkin had gone to her cabin. The next morning, she found the ship was in motion, but she did not find Mr. Peterkin and the little boys at the breakfast-table as usual. She was told that the party who went on shore had all been to the opera, and had returned at a late hour to the steamer, and would naturally be late at breakfast. Mrs. Peterkin went on deck to await them, and look for Malta as it seemed to retreat in the distance. But the day passed on, and neither Mr. Peterkin nor either of the little boys appeared! She tried to calm herself with the thought that they must need sleep; but all the rest of the passengers appeared, relating their different adventures. At last she sent the steward to inquire for them. He came back with one of the officers of the boat, much disturbed, to say that they could not be found; they must have been left behind. There was great excitement, and deep interest expressed for Mrs. Peterkin. One of the officers was very surly, and declared he could not be responsible for the inanity of passengers. Another was more courteous. Mrs. Peterkin asked if they could not go back,—if, at least, she could not be put back. He explained how this would be impossible, but that the company would telegraph when they reached Alexandria.

Mrs. Peterkin calmed herself as well as she could, though indeed she was bewildered by her position. She was to land in Alexandria alone, and the landing she was told would be especially difficult. The steamer would not be able to approach the shore; the passengers would go down the sides of the ship, and be lifted off the steps, by Arabs, into a felucca (whatever that was) below. She shuddered at the prospect. It was darker than her gloomiest fancies had pictured. Would it not be better to remain in the ship, go back to Southampton, perhaps meet Elizabeth Eliza there, picking up Mr. Peterkin at Malta on the way? But at this moment she discovered that she was not on a "P. & O." steamer,—it was a French steamer of the "Messagerie" line; they had stopped at Messina, and not at Malta. She could not go back to Southampton, so she was told by an English colonel on his way to India. He indeed was very courteous, and advised her to "go to an hotel" at Alexandria with some of the ladies, and send her telegrams from there. To whom, however, would she wish to send a telegram?

"Who is Mr. Peterkin's banker?" asked the Colonel. Alas! Mrs. Peterkin did not know. He had at first selected a banker in London, but had afterward changed his mind and talked of a banker in Paris; and she was not sure what was his final decision. She had known the name of the London banker, but had forgotten it, because she had written it down, and she never did remember the things she wrote down in her book. That was her old memorandum-book, and she had left it at home because she had brought a new one for her travels. She was sorry now she had not kept the old book. This, however, was not of so much importance, as it did not contain the name of the Paris banker; and this she had never heard. "Elizabeth Eliza would know;" but how could she reach Elizabeth Eliza?

Some one asked if there were not some friend in America to whom she could appeal, if she did not object to using the ocean telegraph.

"There is a friend in America," said Mrs. Peterkin, "to whom we all of us do go for advice, and who always does help us. She lives in Philadelphia."

"Why not telegraph to her for advice?" asked her friends.

Mrs. Peterkin gladly agreed that it would be the best plan. The expense of the cablegram would be nothing in comparison with the assistance the answer would bring.

Her new friends then invited her to accompany them to their hotel in Alexandria, from which she could send her despatch. The thought of thus being able to reach her hand across the sea to the lady from Philadelphia gave Mrs. Peterkin fresh courage,—courage even to make the landing. As she descended the side of the ship and was guided down the steps, she closed her eyes that she might not see herself lifted into the many-oared boat by the wild-looking Arabs, of whom she had caught a glimpse from above. But she could not close her ears; and as they approached the shore, strange sounds almost deafened her. She closed her eyes again, as she was lifted from the boat and heard the wild yells and shrieks around her. There was a clashing of brass, a jingling of bells, and the screams grew more and more terrific. If she did open her eyes, she saw wild figures gesticulating, dark faces, gay costumes, crowds of men and boys, donkeys, horses, even camels, in the distance. She closed her eyes once more as she was again lifted. Should she now find herself on the back of one of those high camels? Perhaps for this she came to Egypt. But when she looked round again, she found she was leaning back in a comfortable open carriage, with a bottle of salts at her nose. She was in the midst of a strange whirl of excitement; but all the party were bewildered, and she had scarcely recovered her composure when they reached the hotel.

Here a comfortable meal and rest somewhat restored them. By the next day a messenger from the boat brought her the return telegram from Messina. Mr. Peterkin and family, left behind by the "Messagerie" steamer, had embarked the next day by steamer, probably for Naples.

More anxious than ever was Mrs. Peterkin to send her despatch. It was too late the day of their arrival; but at an early hour next day it was sent, and after a day had elapsed, the answer came:—

"All meet at the Sphinx."

Everything now seemed plain. The words were few but clear. Her English friends were going directly to Cairo, and she accompanied them.

After reaching Cairo, the whole party were obliged to rest awhile. They would indeed go with Mrs. Peterkin on her first visit to the Sphinx, as to see the Sphinx and ascend the pyramid formed part of their programme. But many delays occurred to detain them, and Mrs. Peterkin had resolved to carry out completely the advice of the telegram. She would sit every day before the Sphinx. She found that as yet there was no hotel exactly in front of the Sphinx, nor indeed on that side of the river, and she would be obliged to make the excursion of nine miles there and nine miles back, each day. But there would always be a party of travellers whom she could accompany. Each day she grew more and more accustomed to the bewildering sights and sounds about her, and more and more willing to intrust herself to the dark-colored guides. At last, chafing at so many delays, she decided to make the expedition without her new friends. She had made some experiments in riding upon a donkey, and found she was seldom thrown, and could not be hurt by the slight fall.

And so, one day, Mrs. Peterkin sat alone in front of the Sphinx,—alone, as far as her own family and friends were concerned, and yet not alone indeed. A large crowd of guides sat around this strange lady who proposed to spend the day in front of the Sphinx. Clad in long white robes, with white turbans crowning their dark faces, they gazed into her eyes with something of the questioning expression with which she herself was looking into the eyes of the Sphinx.

There were other travellers wandering about. Just now her own party had collected to eat their lunch together; but they were scattered again, and she sat with a circle of Arabs about her, the watchful dragoman lingering near.

Somehow the Eastern languor must have stolen upon her, or she could not have sat so calmly, not knowing where a single member of her family was at that moment. And she had dreaded Egypt so; had feared separation; had even been a little afraid of the Sphinx, upon which she was now looking as at a protecting angel. But they all were to meet at the Sphinx!

If only she could have seen where the different members of the family were at that moment, she could not have sat so quietly. She little knew that a tall form, not far away (following some guides down into the lower halls of a lately excavated temple), with a blue veil wrapped about a face shielded with smoke-colored spectacles, was that of Elizabeth Eliza herself, from whom she had been separated two weeks before.

She little knew that at this moment Solomon John was standing looking over the edge of the Matterhorn, wishing he had not come up so high. But such a gay young party had set off that morning from the hotel that he had supposed it an easy thing to join them; and now he would fain go back, but was tied to the rest of his party with their guide preceding them, and he must keep on and crawl up behind them, still farther, on hands and knees.

Agamemnon was at Mycenæ, looking down into an open pit.

Two of the little boys were roasting eggs in the crater of Mount Vesuvius.

And she would have seen Mr. Peterkin comfortably reclining in a gondola, with one of the little boys, in front of the palaces of Venice.

But none of this she saw; she only looked into the eyes of the Sphinx.

VII.

MRS. PETERKIN FAINTS ON THE GREAT PYRAMID.

"Meet at the Sphinx!" Yes; these were the words that the lady from Philadelphia had sent in answer to the several telegrams that had reached her from each member of the Peterkin family. She had received these messages while staying in a remote country town, but she could communicate with the cable line by means of the telegraph office at a railway station. The intelligent operator, seeing the same date affixed at the close of each message, "took in," as she afterward expressed it, that it was the date of the day on which the message was sent; and as this was always prefixed to every despatch, she did not add it to the several messages. She afterward expressed herself as sorry for the mistake, and declared it should not occur another time.

Elizabeth Eliza was the first at the appointed spot, as her route had been somewhat shorter than the one her mother had taken. A wild joy had seized her when she landed in Egypt, and saw the frequent and happy use of the donkey as a beast of travel. She had never ventured to ride at home, and had always shuddered at the daring of the women who rode at the circuses, and closed her eyes at their performances. But as soon as she saw the little Egyptian donkeys, a mania for riding possessed her. She was so tall that she could scarcely, under any circumstances, fall from them, while she could mount them with as much ease as she could the arm of the sofa at home, and most of the animals seemed as harmless. It is true, the donkey-boys gave her the wrong word to use when she might wish to check the pace of her donkey, and mischievously taught her to avoid the soothing phrase of *beschwesch*, giving her instead one that should goad the beast she rode to its highest speed; but Elizabeth Eliza was so delighted with the quick pace that she was continually urging her donkey onward, to the surprise and delight of each fresh attendant donkey-boy. He would run at a swift pace after her, stopping sometimes to pick up a loose slipper, if it were shuffled off from his foot in his quick run, but always bringing up even in the end.

Elizabeth Eliza's party had made a quick journey by the route from Brindisi, and proceeding directly to Cairo, had stopped at a small French hotel not very far from Mrs. Peterkin and her party. Every morning at an early hour Elizabeth Eliza made her visit to the Sphinx, arriving there always the first one of her own party, and spending the rest of the day in explorations about the neighborhood.

EVERY MORNING AT AN EARLY HOUR ELIZABETH ELIZA
MADE HER VISIT TO THE SPHINX.

Mrs. Peterkin, meanwhile, set out each day at a later hour, arriving in time to take her noon lunch in front of the Sphinx, after which she indulged in a comfortable nap and returned to the hotel before sunset.

A week—indeed, ten days—passed in this way. One morning, Mrs. Peterkin and her party had taken the ferry-boat to cross the Nile. As they were leaving the boat on the other side, in the usual crowd, Mrs. Peterkin's attention was arrested by a familiar voice. She turned, to see a tall young man who, though he wore a red fez upon his head and a scarlet wrap around his neck, certainly resembled Agamemnon. But this Agamemnon was talking Greek, with gesticulations. She was so excited that she turned to follow him through the crowd, thus separating herself from the rest of her party. At once she found herself surrounded by a mob of Arabs, in every kind of costume, all screaming and yelling in the manner to which she was becoming accustomed.

Poor Mrs. Peterkin plaintively protested in English, exclaiming, "I should prefer a donkey!" but the Arabs could not understand her strange words. They had, however, struck the ear of the young man in the red fez whom she had been following. He turned, and she gazed at him. It was Agamemnon!

He, meanwhile, was separated from his party, and hardly knew how to grapple with the urgent Arabs. His recently acquired Greek did not assist him, and he was advising his mother to yield and mount one of the steeds, while he followed on another, when, happily, the dragoman of her party appeared. He administered a volley of rebukes to the persistent Arabs, and bore Mrs. Peterkin to her donkey. She was thus carried away from Agamemnon, who was also mounted upon a donkey by his companions. But their destination was the same; and though they could hold no conversation on the way, Agamemnon could join his mother as they approached the Sphinx.

But he and his party were to ascend the pyramid before going on to the Sphinx, and he advised his mother to do the same. He explained that it was a perfectly easy thing to do. You had only to lift one of your feet up quite high, as though you were going to step on the mantelpiece, and an Arab on each side would lift you to the next step. Mrs. Peterkin was sure she could not step up on their mantelpieces at home. She never had done it,—she never had even tried to. But Agamemnon reminded her that those in their own house were very high,—"old colonial;" and meanwhile she found herself carried along with the rest of the party.

At first the ascent was delightful to her. It seemed as if she were flying. The powerful Nubian guides, one on each side, lifted her jauntily up, without her being conscious of motion. Having seen them daily for some time past, she was now not much afraid of these handsome athletes, with their polished black skins, set off by dazzling white garments. She called out to Agamemnon, who had preceded her, that it was charming; she was not at all afraid. Every now and then she stopped to rest on the broad cornice made by each retreating step. Suddenly, when she was about half-way up, as she leaned back against the step above, she found herself panting and exhausted. A strange faintness came over her. She was looking off over a beautiful scene: through the wide Libyan desert the blue Nile wound between borders of green edging, while the picturesque minarets of Cairo, on the opposite side of the river, and the sand in the distance beyond, gleamed with a red and yellow light beneath the rays of the noonday sun.

But the picture danced and wavered before her dizzy sight. She sat there alone; for Agamemnon and the rest had passed on, thinking she was stopping to rest. She seemed deserted, save by the speechless black statues, one on either side, who, as she seemed to be fainting before their eyes, were looking at her in some anxiety. She saw dimly these wild men gazing at her. She thought of Mungo Park, dying with the African women singing about him. How little she had ever dreamed, when she read that account in her youth, and gazed at the savage African faces in the picture, that she might be left to die in the same way alone, in a strange land—and on the side of a pyramid! Her guides were kindly. One of them took her shawl to wrap about her, as she seemed to be shivering; and as a party coming down from the top had a jar of water, one of her Nubians moistened a handkerchief with water and laid it upon her head. Mrs. Peterkin had closed her eyes, but she opened them again, to see the black figures in their white draperies still standing by her. The travellers coming down paused a few minutes to wonder and give counsel, then passed on, to make way for another party following them. Again Mrs. Peterkin closed her eyes, but once more opened them at hearing a well-known shout,—such a shout as only one of the Peterkin family could give,—one of the little boys!

Yes, he stood before her, and Agamemnon was behind; they had met on top of the pyramid.

The sight was indeed a welcome one to Mrs. Peterkin, and revived her so that she even began to ask questions: "Where had he come from? Where were the other little boys? Where was Mr. Peterkin?" No one could tell where the other little boys were. And the sloping side of the pyramid, with a fresh party waiting to pass up and the guides eager to go down, was not just the place to explain the long, confused story. All that Mrs. Peterkin could understand was that Mr. Peterkin was now, probably, inside the pyramid, beneath her very feet! Agamemnon had found this solitary "little boy" on top of the pyramid, accompanied by a guide and one of the party that he and his father had joined on leaving Venice. At the foot of the pyramid there had been some dispute in the party as to whether they should first go up the pyramid, or down inside, and in the altercation the party was divided; the little boy had been sure that his father meant to go up first, and so he had joined the guide who went up. But where was Mr. Peterkin? Probably in the innermost depths of the pyramid below. As soon as Mrs. Peterkin understood this, she was eager to go down, in spite of her late faintness; even to tumble down would help her to meet Mr. Peterkin the sooner. She was lifted from stone to stone by the careful Nubians. Agamemnon had already emptied his pocket of coins, in supplying backsheesh to his guide, and all were anxious to reach the foot of the pyramid and find the dragoman, who could answer the demands of the others.

Breathless as she was, as soon as she had descended, Mrs. Peterkin was anxious to make for the entrance to the inside. Before, she had declared that nothing would induce her to go into the pyramid. She was afraid of being lost in its stairways and shut up forever as a mummy. But now she forgot all her terrors; she must find Mr. Peterkin at once!

She was the first to plunge down the narrow stairway after the guide, and was grateful to find the steps so easy to descend. But they presently came out into a large, open room, where no stairway was to be seen. On the contrary, she was invited to mount the shoulders of a burly Nubian, to reach a large hole half-way up the side-wall (higher than any mantelpiece), and to crawl through this hole along the passage till she should reach another stairway. Mrs. Peterkin paused. Could she trust these men? Was not this a snare to entice her into one of these narrow passages? Agamemnon was far behind. Could Mr. Peterkin have ventured into this treacherous place?

At this moment a head appeared through the opening above, followed by a body. It was that of one of the native guides. Voices were heard coming through the passage: one voice had a twang to it that surely Mrs. Peterkin had heard before. Another head appeared now, bound with a blue veil, while the eyes were hidden by green goggles. Yet Mrs. Peterkin could not be mistaken, —it was—yes, it was the head of Elizabeth Eliza!

It seemed as though that were all, it was so difficult to bring forward any more of her. Mrs. Peterkin was screaming from below, asking if it were indeed Elizabeth Eliza, while excitement at recognizing her mother made it more difficult for Elizabeth Eliza to extricate herself. But travellers below and behind urged her on, and with the assistance of the guides, she pushed forward and almost fell into the arms of her mother. Mrs. Peterkin was wild with joy as Agamemnon and his brother joined them.

"But Mr. Peterkin!" at last exclaimed their mother. "Did you see anything of your father?"

"He is behind," said Elizabeth Eliza. "I was looking for the body of Chufu, the founder of the pyramid,—for I have longed to be the discoverer of his mummy,—and I found instead—my father!"

Mrs. Peterkin looked up, and at that moment saw Mr. Peterkin emerging from the passage above. He was carefully planting one foot on the shoulder of a stalwart Nubian guide. He was very red in the face, from recent exertion, but he was indeed Mr. Peterkin. On hearing the cry of Mrs. Peterkin, he tottered, and would have fallen but for the support of the faithful guide.

The narrow place was scarcely large enough to hold their joy. Mrs. Peterkin was ready to faint again with her great excitement. She wanted to know what had become of the other little boys, and if Mr. Peterkin had heard from Solomon John. But the small space was becoming more and more crowded. The dragomans from the different parties with which the Peterkins were connected came to announce their several luncheons, and insisted upon their leaving the pyramid.

Mrs. Peterkin's dragoman wanted her to go on directly to the Sphinx, and she still clung to the belief that only then would there be a complete reunion of the family. Yet she could not separate herself from the rest. They could not let her go, and they were all hungry, and she herself felt the need of food.

But with the confusion of so many luncheons, and so much explanation to be gone through with, it was difficult to get an answer to her questions.

Elizabeth and her father were involved in a discussion as to whether they should have met if he had not gone into the queen's chamber in the pyramid. For if he had not gone to the queen's chamber he would have left the inside of the pyramid before Mrs. Peterkin reached it, and would have missed her, as he was too fatigued to make the ascent. And Elizabeth Eliza, if she had not met her father, had planned going back to the king's chamber in another search for the body of Chufu, in which case she would have been too late to meet her mother. Mrs. Peterkin was not much interested in this discussion; it was enough that they had met. But she could not get answers to what she considered more important questions; while Elizabeth Eliza, though delighted to meet again her father and mother and brothers, and though interested in the fate of the missing ones, was absorbed in the Egyptian question; and the mingling of all their interests made satisfactory intercourse impracticable.

Where was Solomon John? What had become of the body of Chufu? Had Solomon John been telegraphed to? When had Elizabeth Eliza seen him last? Was he Chufu or Shufu, and why Cheops? and where were the other little boys?

Mr. Peterkin attempted to explain that he had taken a steamer from Messina to the south of Italy, and a southern route to Brindisi. By mistake he had taken the steamer from Alexandria, on its way to Venice, instead of the one that was leaving Brindisi for Alexandria at the same hour. Indeed, just as he had discovered his mistake, and had seen the other boat steaming off by his side in the other direction, too late he fancied he saw the form of Elizabeth Eliza on deck, leaning over the taffrail (if it was a taffrail). It was a tall lady, with a blue veil wound around her hat. Was it possible? Could he have been in time to reach Elizabeth Eliza? His explanation only served to increase the number of questions.

Mrs. Peterkin had many more. How had Agamemnon reached them? Had he come to Bordeaux with them? But Agamemnon and Elizabeth Eliza were now discussing with others the number of feet that the Great Pyramid measured. The remaining members of all the parties, too, whose hunger and thirst were now fully satisfied, were ready to proceed to the Sphinx, which only Mrs. Peterkin and Elizabeth Eliza had visited.

Side by side on their donkeys, Mrs. Peterkin attempted to learn something from Mr. Peterkin about the other little boys. But his donkey proved restive: now it bore him on in swift flight from Mrs. Peterkin; now it would linger behind. His words were jerked out only at intervals. All that could be said was that they were separated; the little boys wanted to go to Vesuvius, but Mr. Peterkin felt they must hurry to Brindisi. At a station where the two trains parted—one for Naples, the other for Brindisi—he found suddenly, too late, that they were not with him; they must have gone on to Naples. But where were they now?

VIII.

THE LAST OF THE PETERKINS.

The expedition up the Nile had taken place successfully. The Peterkin family had reached Cairo again,—at least, its scattered remnant was there, and they were now to consider what next.

Mrs. Peterkin would like to spend her life in the dahabieh,[1] though she could not pronounce its name, and she still felt the strangeness of the scenes about her. However, she had only to look out upon the mud villages on the bank to see that she was in the veritable "Africa" she had seen pictured in the geography of her childhood. If further corroboration were required, had she not, only the day before, when accompanied by no one but a little donkey-boy, shuddered to meet a strange Nubian, attired principally in hair that stood out from his savage face in frizzes at least half a yard long?

But oh the comforts of no trouble in housekeeping on board the dahabieh! Never to know what they were to have for dinner, nor to be asked what they would like, and yet always to have a dinner you could ask chance friends to, knowing all would be perfectly served! Some of the party with whom they had engaged their dahabieh had even brought canned baked beans from New England, which seemed to make their happiness complete.

"Though we see beans here," said Mrs. Peterkin, "they are not 'Boston beans'!"

She had fancied she would have to live on stuffed ostrich (ostrich stuffed with iron filings, that the books tell of), or fried hippopotamus, or boiled rhinoceros. But she met with none of these, and day after day was rejoiced to find her native turkey appearing on the table, with pigeons and chickens (though the chickens, to be sure, were scarcely larger than the pigeons), and lamb that was really not more tough than that of New Hampshire and the White Mountains.

If they dined with the Arabs, there was indeed a kind of dark molasses-gingerbread-looking cake, with curds in it, that she found it hard to eat. "But *they* like it," she said complacently.

The remaining little boy, too, smiled over his pile of ripe bananas, as he thought of the quarter-of-a-dollar-a-half-dozen green ones at that moment waiting at the corners of the streets at home. Indeed, it was a land for boys. There were the dates, both fresh and dried,—far more juicy than those learned at school; and there was the gingerbread-nut tree, the dôm palm, that bore a nut tasting "like baker's gingerbread that has been kept a few days in the shop," as the remaining little boy remarked. And he wished for his brothers when the live dinner came on board their boat, at the stopping-places, in the form of good-sized sheep struggling on the shoulders of stout Arabs, or an armful of live hens and pigeons.

All the family (or as much of it as was present) agreed with Mrs. Peterkin's views. Amanda at home had seemed quite a blessing, but at this distance her services, compared with the attentions of their Maltese dragoman and the devotion of their Arab servants, seemed of doubtful value, and even Mrs. Peterkin dreaded returning to her tender mercies.

"Just imagine inviting the Russian Count to dinner at home—and Amanda!" exclaimed Elizabeth Eliza.

"And he came to dinner at least three times a week on board the boat," said the remaining little boy.

"The Arabs are so convenient about carrying one's umbrellas and shawls," said Elizabeth Eliza. "How I should miss Hassan in picking up my blue veil!"

The family recalled many anecdotes of the shortcomings of Amanda, as Mrs. Peterkin leaned back upon her divan and wafted a fly-whisk. Mr. Peterkin had expended large sums in telegrams from every point where he found the telegraph in operation; but there was no reply from Solomon John, and none from the two little boys.

By a succession of telegrams they had learned that no one had fallen into the crater of Vesuvius in the course of the last six months, not even a little boy. This was consoling.

By letters from the lady from Philadelphia, they learned that she had received Solomon John's telegram from Geneva at the time she heard from the rest of the family, and one signed "L. Boys" from Naples. But neither of these telegrams gave an address for return answers, which she had, however, sent to Geneva and Naples, with the fatal omission by the operator (as she afterward learned) of the date, as in the other telegrams.

Mrs. Peterkin therefore disliked to be long away from the Sphinx, and their excursion up the Nile had been shortened on this account. All the Nubian guides near the pyramids had been furnished with additional backsheesh and elaborate explanations from Mr. Peterkin as to how they should send him information if Solomon John and the little boys should turn up at the Sphinx, —for all the family agreed they would probably appear in Egypt together.

Mrs. Peterkin regretted not having any photographs to leave with the guides; but Elizabeth Eliza, alas! had lost at Brindisi the hand-bag that contained the family photograph-book.

Mrs. Peterkin would have liked to take up her residence near the Sphinx for the rest of the year. But every one warned her that the heat of an Egyptian summer would not allow her to stay at Cairo,—scarcely even on the sea-shore, at Alexandria.

How thankful was Mrs. Peterkin, a few months after, when the war in Egypt broke out, that her wishes had not been yielded to! For many nights she could not sleep, picturing how they all might have been massacred by the terrible mob in Alexandria.

Intelligence of Solomon John led them to take their departure.

One day, they were discussing at the *table d'hôte* their letters from the lady from Philadelphia, and how they showed that Solomon John had been at Geneva.

"Ah, there was his mistake!" said Elizabeth Eliza. "The Doolittles left Marseilles with us, and were to branch off for Geneva, and we kept on to Genoa, and Solomon John was always mistaking Genoa for Geneva, as we planned our route. I remember there was a great confusion when they got off."

"I always mix up Geneva and Genoa," said Mrs. Peterkin. "I feel as if they were the same."

"They are quite different," said Elizabeth Eliza; "and Genoa lay in our route, while Geneva took him into Switzerland."

An English gentleman, on the opposite side of the table, then spoke to Mr. Peterkin.

"I beg pardon," he said. "I think I met one of your name in Athens. He attracted our attention because he went every day to the same spot, and he told us he expected to meet his family there,—that he had an appointment by telegraph—"

"In Athens!" exclaimed Mrs. Peterkin.

"Was his name Solomon John?" asked Elizabeth Eliza.

"Were there two little boys?" inquired Mrs. Peterkin.

"His initials were the same as mine," replied the Englishman,—"S.J.P.,— for some of his luggage came by mistake into my room, and that is why I spoke of it."

"Is there a Sphinx in Athens?" Mrs. Peterkin inquired.

"There used to be one there," said Agamemnon.

"I beg your pardon," said the Englishman, "but that Sphinx never was in Athens."

"But Solomon John may have made the mistake,—we all make our mistakes," said Mrs. Peterkin, tying her bonnet-strings, as if ready to go to meet Solomon John at that moment.

"The Sphinx was at Thebes in the days of Œdipus," said the Englishman. "No one would expect to find it anywhere in Greece at the present day."

"But was Solomon John inquiring for it?" asked Mr. Peterkin.

"Indeed, no!" answered the Englishman; "he went every day to the Pnyx, a famous hill in Athens, where his telegram had warned him he should meet his friends."

"The Pnyx!" exclaimed Mr. Peterkin; "and how do you spell it?"

"P-n-y-x!" cried Agamemnon,—"the same letters as in Sphinx!"

"All but the *s* and the *h* and the *y*" said Elizabeth Eliza.

"I often spell Sphinx with a *y* myself," said Mr. Peterkin.

"And a telegraph-operator makes such mistakes!" said Agamemnon.

"His telegram had been forwarded to him from Switzerland," said the Englishman; "it had followed him into the dolomite region, and must have been translated many timed."

"And of course they could not all have been expected to keep the letters in the right order," said Elizabeth Eliza.

"And were there two little boys with him?" repeated Mrs. Peterkin.

No; there were no little boys. But further inquiries satisfied the family that Solomon John must be awaiting them in Athens. And how natural the mistake! Mrs. Peterkin said that if she had known of a Pnyx, she should surely have looked for the family there.

Should they then meet Solomon John at the Pnyx, or summon him to Egypt? It seemed safer to go directly to Athens, especially as Mr. Peterkin and Agamemnon were anxious to visit that city.

It was found that a steamer would leave Alexandria next day for Athens, by way of Smyrna and Constantinople. This was a roundabout course; but Mr. Peterkin was impatient to leave, and was glad to gain more acquaintance with the world. Meanwhile they could telegraph their plans to Solomon John, as the English gentleman could give them the address of his hotel.

And Mrs. Peterkin did not now shrink from another voyage. Her experience on the Nile had made her forget her sufferings in crossing the Atlantic, and she no longer dreaded entering another steamboat. Their delight in river navigation, indeed, had been so great that the whole family had listened with interest to the descriptions given by their Russian fellow-traveller of steamboat navigation on the Volga—"the most beautiful river in the world," as he declared. Elizabeth Eliza and Mr. Peterkin were eager to try it, and Agamemnon remarked that such a trip would give them an opportunity to visit the renowned fair at Nijninovgorod. Even Mrs. Peterkin had consented to this expedition, provided they should meet Solomon John and the other little boys.

She started, therefore, on a fresh voyage without any dread, forgetting that the Mediterranean, if not so wide as the Atlantic, is still a sea, and often as tempestuous and uncomfortably "choppy." Alas! she was soon to be awakened from her forgetfulness: the sea was the same old enemy.

As they passed up among the Ionian Isles, and she heard Agamemnon and Elizabeth Eliza and their Russian friend (who was accompanying them to Constantinople) talking of the old gods of Greece, she fancied that they were living still, and that Neptune and the classic waves were wreaking their vengeance on them, and pounding and punishing them for venturing to rule them with steam. She was fairly terrified. As they entered Smyrna she declared she would never enter any kind of a boat again, and that Mr. Peterkin must find some way by which they could reach home by land.

How delightful it was to draw near the shore, on a calm afternoon,—even to trust herself to the charge of the boatmen in leaving the ship, and to reach land once more and meet the tumult of voices and people! Here were the screaming and shouting usual in the East, and the same bright array of turbans and costumes in the crowd awaiting them. But a well-known voice reached them, and from the crowd rose a well-known face. Even before they reached the land they had recognized its owner. With his American dress, he looked almost foreign in contrast to the otherwise universal Eastern color. A tall figure on either side seemed, also, each to have a familiar air.

Were there three Solomon Johns?

No; it was Solomon John and the two other little boys—but grown so that they were no longer little boys. Even Mrs. Peterkin was unable to recognize them at first. But the tones of their voices, their ways, were as natural as ever. Each had a banana in his hand, and pockets stuffed with oranges.

Questions and answers interrupted each other in a most confusing manner:

"Are you the little boys?"

"Where have you been?"

"Did you go to Vesuvius?"

"How did you get away?"

"Why didn't you come sooner?"

"Our India-rubber boots stuck in the hot lava."

"Have you been there all this time?"

"No; we left them there."

"Have you had fresh dates?"

"They are all gone now, but the dried ones are better than those squeezed ones we have at home."

"How you have grown!"

"Why didn't you telegraph?"

"Why did you go to Vesuvius, when Papa said he couldn't?"

"Did you, too, think it was Pnyx?"

"Where have you been all winter?"

"Did you roast eggs in the crater?"

"When did you begin to grow?"

The little boys could not yet thoroughly explain themselves; they always talked together and in foreign languages, interrupting each other, and never agreeing as to dates.

Solomon John accounted for his appearance in Smyrna by explaining that when he received his father's telegram in Athens, he decided to meet them at Smyrna. He was tired of waiting at the Pnyx. He had but just landed, and came near missing his family, and the little boys too, who had reached Athens just as he was leaving it. None of the family wished now to continue their journey to Athens, but they had the advice and assistance of their Russian friend in planning to leave the steamer at Constantinople; they would, by adopting this plan, be *en route* for the proposed excursion to the Volga.

Mrs. Peterkin was overwhelmed with joy at having all her family together once more; but with it a wave of homesickness surged over her. They were all together; why not go home?

It was found that there was a sailing-vessel bound absolutely for Maine, in which they might take passage. No more separation; no more mistakes; no more tedious study of guide-books; no more weighing of baggage. Every trunk and bag, every Peterkin, could be placed in the boat, and safely landed on the shores of home. It was a temptation, and at one time Mrs. Peterkin actually pleaded for it.

But there came a throbbing in her head, a swimming in her eyes, a swaying of the very floor of the hotel. Could she bear it, day after day, week after week? Would any of them be alive? And Constantinople not seen, nor steam-navigation on the Volga!

And so new plans arose, and wonderful discoveries were made, and the future of the Peterkin family was changed forever.

In the first place a strange stout gentleman in spectacles had followed the Peterkin family to the hotel, had joined in the family councils, and had rendered valuable service in negotiating with the officers of the steamer for the cancellation of their through tickets to Athens. He dined at the same table, and was consulted by the (formerly) little boys.

Who was he?

They explained that he was their "preceptor." It appeared that after they parted from their father, the little boys had become mixed up with some pupils who were being taken by their preceptor to Vesuvius. For some time he had not noticed that his party (consisting of boys of their own age) had been enlarged; and after finding this out, he had concluded they were the sons of an English family with whom he had been corresponding. He was surprised that no further intelligence came with them, and no extra baggage. They had, however, their hand-bags; and after sending their telegram to the lady from Philadelphia, they assured him that all would be right. But they were obliged to leave Naples the very day of despatching the telegram, and left no address to which an answer could be sent. The preceptor took them, with his pupils, directly back to his institution in Gratz, Austria, from which he had taken them on this little excursion.

It was not till the end of the winter that he discovered that his youthful charges—whom he had been faithfully instructing, and who had found the gymnasium and invigorating atmosphere so favorable to growth—were not the sons of his English correspondent, whom he had supposed, from their explanations, to be travelling in America.

He was, however, intending to take his pupils to Athens in the spring, and by this time the little boys were able to explain themselves better in his native language. They assured him they should meet their family in the East, and the preceptor felt it safe to take them upon the track proposed.

It was now that Mr. Peterkin prided himself upon the plan he had insisted upon before leaving home. "Was it not well," he exclaimed, "that I provided each of you with a bag of gold, for use in case of emergency, hidden in the lining of your hand-bags?"

This had worked badly for Elizabeth Eliza, to be sure, who had left hers at Brindisi; but the little boys had been able to pay some of their expenses, which encouraged the preceptor to believe he might trust them for the rest. So much pleased were all the family with the preceptor that they decided that all three of the little boys should continue under his instructions, and return with him to Gratz. This decision made more easy the other plans of the family.

Both Agamemnon and Solomon John had decided they would like to be foreign consuls. They did not much care where, and they would accept any appointment; and both, it appeared, had written on the subject to the Department at Washington. Agamemnon had put in a plea for a vacancy at Madagascar, and Solomon John hoped for an opening at Rustchuk, Turkey; if not there, at Aintab, Syria. Answers were expected, which were now telegraphed for, to meet them in Constantinople.

Meanwhile Mr. Peterkin had been consulting the preceptor and the Russian Count about a land-journey home. More and more Mrs. Peterkin determined she could not and would not trust herself to another voyage, though she consented to travel by steamer to Constantinople. If they went as far as Nijninovgorod, which was now decided upon, why could they not persevere through "Russia in Asia"?

Their Russian friend at first shook his head at this, but at last agreed that it might be possible to go on from Novgorod comfortably to Tobolsk, perhaps even from there to Yakoutsk, and then to Kamtschatka.

"And cross at Behring's Strait!" exclaimed Mrs. Peterkin. "It looks so narrow on the map."

"And then we are in Alaska," said Mr. Peterkin.

"And at home," exclaimed Mrs. Peterkin, "and no more voyages."

But Elizabeth Eliza doubted about Kamtschatka and Behring's Strait, and thought it would be very cold.

"But we can buy furs on our way," insisted Mrs. Peterkin.

"And if you do not find the journey agreeable," said their Russian friend, "you can turn back from Yakoutsk, even from Tobolsk, and come to visit us."

Yes—*us*! For Elizabeth Eliza was to marry the Russian Count!

He had been in a boat that was behind them on the Nile, had met them often, had climbed the ruins with them, joined their excursions, and had finally proposed at Edfu.

Elizabeth Eliza had then just written to consult the lady from Philadelphia with regard to the offer of a German professor they had met, and she could give no reply to the Count.

Now, however, it was necessary to make a decision. She had meanwhile learned a few words of Russian. The Count spoke English moderately well, made himself understood better than the Professor, and could understand Elizabeth Eliza's French. Also the Count knew how to decide questions readily, while the Professor had to consider both sides before he could make up his mind.

Mrs. Peterkin objected strongly at first. She could not even pronounce the Russian's name. "How should she be able to speak to him, or tell anybody whom Elizabeth Eliza had married?" But finally the family all gave their consent, won by the attention and devotion of Elizabeth Eliza's last admirer.

The marriage took place in Constantinople, not at Santa Sophia, as Elizabeth Eliza would have wished, as that was under a Mohammedan dispensation. A number of American residents were present, and the preceptor sent for his other pupils in Athens. Elizabeth Eliza wished there was time to invite the lady from Philadelphia to be present, and Ann Maria Bromwick. Would the name be spelled right in the newspapers? All that could be done was to spell it by telegraph as accurately as possible, as far as they themselves knew how, and then leave the papers to do their best (or their worst) in their announcements of the wedding "at the American Consulate, Constantinople, Turkey. No cards."

The last that was ever heard of the Peterkins, Agamemnon was on his way to Madagascar, Solomon John was at Rustchuk, and the little boys at Gratz; Mr. and Mrs. Peterkin, in a comfortable sledge, were on their way from Tobolsk to Yakoutsk; and Elizabeth Eliza was passing her honeymoon in the neighborhood of Moscow.

OTHERS OF THEIR KIN.

IX.

LUCILLA'S DIARY.

MONDAY.—I spent some time this morning watching for the rag-man. I wish I had taken down a note which day it was I saw him before. I remember it was washing-day, for I had to take my hands out of the tub and wipe the suds off when Johnnie came to tell me that the rag-man was on the street. He was just turning the corner by the Wylies when I got to the front gate. But whether we washed on Monday I can't think. It rained that Monday, or the week before, and we had to wait till Tuesday; but which it was I couldn't say. I was in such a whirl fitting Artemas off, and much as ever I made him hear; and he wasn't the right man after all, for he wouldn't give more than a cent and a half a pound for the papers, and Mrs. Carruthers got two cents. She could not remember what was his day for coming, but agreed to send him if she should see him again.

Mrs. Carruthers sent the rag-man to-day; but I can't say much for the bargain, though he was a different man from the one that came Monday, and it seems it was Monday. He agreed to give me the same he gave Mrs. Carruthers,—two cents a pound. And I had a lot of newspapers,—all the papers Artemas has been taking through the winter; for he doesn't like me to take them for kindlings, says he would rather pay separate for kindlings, as I might burn the wrong one. And there were the papers that came around his underclothes and inside the packing boxes he has taken away. So I expected to make something; but he gave me no more than forty-five cents! He weighed them, and said himself there were thirty pounds. That ought to have come to sixty cents at least, according to my arithmetic. But he made out it was all right, and had them all packed up, and went off, though I followed him out to the gate and told him that it didn't amount to no more than I might have got from the other man at a cent and a half. He said it was all they were worth; that he wished he could get as much for them. Then I asked him why he took the trouble to come for them, under the circumstances. But by that time he was off and down the street.

I was just sitting at the window this morning, and there were Mr. and Mrs. Peebles walking down the street,—he on one side and she on the other. I do wonder why they didn't go on the same side! If they hadn't got so far past the gate, I'd have asked them. I never heard there was any quarrel between them, and it was just as muddy this side of the street as that. They have been spending their winters in the city lately, and perhaps it's some new fashion.

I declare it's worth while to sit at the window now and then, and see what is going on. I'm usually so busy at the back of the house, I don't know. But now Lavinia has taken to going to school with the boys, and they are willing to take care of her, half my work seems taken out of my hands. Not that she was much in the way for a girl of four, but she might slip out of the gate at any time, as there are so many of those grinding organs around with their monkeys.

Mrs. Carruthers was in yesterday afternoon, and she said the Peebles were looking up the numbers on the doors to find the Wylies. They got puzzled because the numbers go up one side of the street and down the other, and they haven't but just been put on. And it seems that up in the city they have them go across. It does appear to me shiftless in our town officers, when they undertook to have the streets numbered as they do elsewhere, that they didn't number them the same way. But I can't see but our way is as good, and more sensible than having to cross a muddy street to look up the next number.

Artemas has been gone a whole week. I told him I would put down the most important things in a diary, and then he can look at it, if he has time, when he comes home. He thinks it is a more sensible way than writing letters every week.

He expects to be up and down in Texas, and perhaps across the mountains; and in those lawless countries letters would not stand much chance,—maybe they wouldn't ever reach him, after I'd had the trouble of writing them. There's the expense of stamps too,—not so very much for one letter, but it counts up.

Nothing worries me more than getting a letter, unless it's having a telegraph come,—and that does give one a start. But even that's sooner over and quicker read; while for a letter, it's long, and it takes a good while to get to the end. I feel it might be a kind of waste of time to write in my diary; but not more than writing letters, and it saves the envelopes and hunting them up. I'm not likely to find much time for either, for the boys are fairly through their winter suits; if I can only keep them along while the spring hangs off so.

Mrs. Norris was in yesterday, just as I was writing about the boys' suits, to know if I would let Martha off to work for her after the washing is over. I told her I didn't like to disoblige, but I couldn't see my way clear to get along without Martha. The boys ought to be having their spring suits this very minute, and Martha was calculating to make them this week; and they'd have to have their first wear of them Sundays for a while before they start on them for school. I never was so behindhand; but what with fitting off Artemas and the spring cleaning being delayed, I didn't seem to know how to manage. Martha is good at making over, and there are two very good coats of Artemas's that she would do the right thing by; while there was a good many who could scrub and clean as well as she,—there was that Nora that used to live at Patty's. But Mrs. Norris did not take to Nora. The Wylies tried her, but could make nothing out of her. I said I thought it would be hard to find the person Mrs. Wylie could get on with. Not that I ever knew anything about her till she came to live on our street last winter, but they do say she's just as hard on her own family; for there's a story that she won't let that pretty daughter of hers, Clara, marry Bob Prince's son, Larkin.

Mrs. Norris said she didn't wonder, for Larkin Prince hadn't found anything to do since he came home. I thought there was enough to live upon in the Wylie family, even if Larkin didn't find something the first minute he'd got his education.

I can see that Mrs. Norris didn't take it well that I was not willing to give up Martha; but I don't really see why I should be the one to give up. But I must say I haven't got on as well with the work as I had hoped, Lavinia's going with the boys so much keeps her clothes half torn off her back, and I can't seem to see how to make her tidy. I was real ashamed when I went to lift her out of a mud-puddle yesterday outside the gate; and there was Clara Wylie looking as clean as a white lily, and she stopped to help her out. It seemed that Lavinia had left her boot in the last mud-puddle, and I would have liked to have gone through the ground. I hope it will be a lesson to Lavinia, for Miss Wylie oughtn't to have touched her with her hand. But she did, yellow gloves and all, and said it was dreadful walking now, the frost so late coming out of the ground, and she had quite envied Lavinia running across the fields after the boys. But Lavinia has taken to envying Miss Wylie, and wishes she could wear that kind of boots she has, with high heels that keep her out of the mud-puddles.

I am thinking of having my ruby cashmere colored over. I don't seem to feel like ripping it all up, pleatings and all; but Mrs. Peebles says it can be dipped just as well made up, and I needn't take out a seam. I might have it a kind of dark olive, like Mrs. Carruthers' dress.

I have had a start! It is a letter from Artemas; nothing particular about himself, only I should say he was well. But he wants to take out a young man farther west with him,—somebody with something of an education, who understands chemicals or engineering, and he wants me to pick out somebody. There's my brother Sam, of course. I thought of him the first thing. But Artemas never took to Sam, though he is my brother. Still, I dare say he would do right by him. And Sam don't seem to find the work here that suits, and I hate to have him hanging round. But he don't know more than I about chemicals, as much as even what they are, though I dare say he could find out, for Sam is smart and always could make out if he chose to lay his hands to anything. And I dare say Artemas thought of Sam, and that is why he sent to me to give him a chance. From what he says it must be a pretty good chance, exactly what Sam would like if he knew anything about the business. I dare say he'd do quite as well as half the fellows who might go. He can be steady if he's a mind to.

But I can't but think of Larkin Prince; how he's taken all the pains to get an education, and his father for him laying up money for the very purpose, and that pretty Clara Wylie waiting to be married till he should get something fit to do, and maybe her father wanting to marry her off to some rich man while she's waiting, when her heart is set on Larkin. And he'd be just the man for Artemas, seeing as he's been studying just such things.

It wasn't no use taking up the time writing in my diary, as Artemas must have a telegraph before night, and the boys home from school to know if they might go to the swamp after checkerberries, and Lavinia with them, and I let her go, clean apron and all, and I put on my bonnet to go over to Mrs. Prince's. It made my heart bump to think how much Sam would set on having the situation, and Artemas kind of expecting him; but I said to myself, if Larkin should be out of town, or anything, that would settle the matter for Sam.

As it happened, who should I meet but Larkin just at the gate! and I asked him if he would turn back and step in with me for a minute. He looked kind of provoked, and I shouldn't wonder if he hadn't expected to meet Clara Wylie coming out of her gate just below, as it's natural she should at this time. But he came in, and I gave him Artemas's letter to read, for there wasn't anything in it except particulars of the work. He quite started as he read it, and then he looked at me inquiring, and I asked him if he had the kind of knowledge Artemas wanted. I supposed he might have it, as he'd been to the new schools. It told in the letter about the expenses, and what the pay would be, and where he would find the free pass, and that he'd have to telegraph right off, and perhaps he noticed he'd have to start to-night. Well, I guess he needn't care even to thank me; for that look in his face was enough, and I shan't forget it. He wanted to know was it Artemas thought of him. But before I could answer, he saw somebody out in the street, and went to rushing out, only he gave me another of those looks as he went, and said he'd see me before he sent the telegraph, and would take any message from me to Artemas.

I hadn't more than time to write this yesterday, when Mrs. Norris came in to inquire about some garden seeds, but I guess she expected to find out what Larkin Prince had been in for, for she was calling over at Mrs. Carruthers'. I offered her some squash seeds, and took her out the back way, through the garden, to show her how the squashes were likely to spread. Last summer they were all over the garden. It seems the only thing the boys let to grow.

She hadn't more than gone when Larkin came in. It was all settled, and other things seemed to be settled too; for who should come in with him but Clara Wylie, crying and smiling all at once. She had to come and help Larkin to thank me because he had got the place. After he was gone she came back for a little cry. She didn't seem to wonder that Larkin was the one chosen, and supposed Artemas must have known all about him, she said, as well as the company he is working for. They probably had seen his name in the papers, she thought, when he graduated so honorably from the school.

I didn't tell her that there wasn't any company; that Artemas never had time to read that kind of thing in the newspapers, and would not have noticed it if he had; and that he'd left it all to me.

I can't but say after it was all settled I had a kind of a turn myself, to think that Sam might have gone just as well, and I had been standing in his way.

I shall have to let down Lavinia's gowns full two inches this summer. Lucky I put tucks in them all last year. Mrs. Carruthers wanted me to finish them off with a frill; lucky I didn't, it would have been up to her ears this summer. As for the boys, I can take them in turn,—last year's clothes for the next boy all the way down, and Cyrus can have his father's. But it seems harder to fit out Lavinia. The ruby cashmere is as good for me as new; it is dipped.

I'm real sorry about the Jones's losing their cow; it comes hard for them. It's better for our potato patch, particularly if they do not have another. Cyrus ought to fence it in.

Sam came in last night. He had heard that Larkin Prince was summoned off by a company out West, for work that would pay, and would set him up for years, and he had a free pass, and old Wylie had given his consent to his marrying Clara. Some people, he said, had luck come to them without trying for it, just standing round. There was he himself had been looking for just such work last year, and nobody had thought of him.

I hope I wasn't hard on Sam. I couldn't help telling him if he'd gone up to the schools, as Larkin Prince did, and he might have done, he could have made himself fit for an engineer or a chemical agent. Well, it took him kind of surprised, and I agreed to go round this evening, when father is at home, and talk to father and mother about Sam's going to some of them schools. At least he might try; and, anyhow, it would get him out of the kind of company he's taken a fancy to.

I must say I didn't think of how he'd feel about Clara Wylie; but, of course, her father would never have given Sam any encouragement more than Larkin. And as for Clara Wylie—well, I saw her look at Larkin that night.

I don't know but I made a mistake in sending so many of his woollen socks to Artemas by Larkin Prince. Perhaps I had better have sent more of the cotton ones. Larkin said he would tell him we were all well, and how he found us. Lavinia had gone up to bed, and was hollering to me to come up to her, and Cyrus slung Silas's cap into the window, and it most hit Larkin; Silas came in after it through the window, and the rest of the boys were pounding on the barn door, where they were having a militia meeting, or some kind of a parade, with half the boys in town. So Artemas will know things goes on about as usual.

An excellent sermon from Mr. Jenkins today. I can't seem to think what it was about, to put it down; but we are all of us more and more pleased with him as a minister. You can't expect all things of any man; and if a minister preaches a good sermon twice a Sunday and perhaps at evening meeting, and goes around among the people as much as Mr. Jenkins, and holds meetings through the week, and Bible class every Friday evening, and sits by the bedside of the sick and the dying, and gives a hand in his own farming or a neighbor's, and stands on the committee for the schools, I don't know as you can expect much more of him.

Mrs. Carruthers says there's a talk of the Peebles moving up to the city for good and all. I should think they might as well go as careening back and forth, spring and fall; though she says they will still go down to the seashore or up to the mountains, summers. When I had a home, I will say, I liked to stay in it.

There, now! I do believe that I have not mentioned in my diary that our house is burned down, and much as ever we all got out alive, coming in the night so. I suppose I ought to have put it in as being one of the principal events; but somehow I have been so unsettled since the fire, I haven't seemed to think to write it down. And, of course, Artemas would see from the depot, the minute he arrived, that the house wasn't there, and he wouldn't need to wait and read about it in my diary; and I have been pretty busy getting set to rights again. Everything being burnt, there 's all the summer clothes to be made over again, except a few things I brought off in a bundle along with the diary. Still, it might have been better than writing about my neighbors, as I did about the Peebles.

Mr. Jenkins came in as I was writing. He says that diaries are good things, and if you didn't put in only your thoughts in a sentimental kind of way, they'd be useful for posterity. I told him I didn't write for posterity, but for Artemas, instead of a letter. He was surprised I hadn't written him about the fire, as the news might reach him exaggerated. I could not help from laughing, for I don't see how it could be made out much worse,—the house burnt down, and the barn with the horse in it, and Cyrus's crop of squashes. Much as ever we got out alive, and I had to come to rooms—two pair, back. I did bring the diary out in my apron.

Mr. Jenkins spoke of the insurance, and maybe Artemas might have something to say about that; but we talked it all over the night before he went away, and he spoke of the insurance being out, and he didn't think it worth while to renew; there never had been a fire, and it wasn't likely there would be.

Mrs. Carruthers came in to inquire when was a good time to try out soap. I told her I managed generally to do it when Artemas wasn't at home, as he was not partial to the smell in the house. But Mr. Carruthers never does go away, and she doesn't believe he'd notice it. I don't know but I'd rather have my husband coming and going like Artemas, instead of sticking around not noticing, especially if he was Mr. Carruthers.

Clara Wylie has been with letters in her hands, and it seems she wrote to Larkin Prince all about our fire; how our boys dropped matches in the hay, and the fire spread to the house from the barn, and how we were waked up, and had to hurry out just as we were. I don't believe she told how the Wylies took us in that night, and found us these rooms at their aunt Marshall's till Artemas comes home. But it seems that Artemas has told Larkin it ain't no kind of consequence, the house burning down, because he never liked it facing the depot, and he'll be glad to build again, and has money enough for it, and can satisfy the neighbors if there's a complaint that our boys burned down all that side of the street, with being careless with their matches. And there was a note inclosed to me from Artemas. He says he'd had a kind of depressed time, when things were going wrong, but matters began to look up when Larkin Prince came, who had just the information needed. So it's just as well I didn't write about the fire. I hope Artemas don't talk too large about his earning so much; anyhow, I shall try to get along spending next to nothing, and earning what I can making buttonholes.

I've made over my ruby cashmere for Lavinia, and I'm sorry now that I had it dyed over so dark, the olive is kind of dull for her; but I can't seem to lay my hand on anything else for her, and she must have something. Lucky it was lying on the chair, close by the door, so I brought it off from the fire.

Artemas has come home.

X.

JEDIDIAH'S NOAH'S ARK.

I.

"I don't see how we can ever get them back again," said Mr. Dyer.

"Why should not we ask the 'grateful people'?" asked Jedidiah.

To explain what Jedidiah and his father meant, I shall have to tell how it was Jedidiah came to have a Noah's Ark, and all about it, for it was a little odd.

Jedidiah was the son of poor parents. His father lived in a small, neat house, and owned a little farm. It was not much of a place; but he worked hard, and raised vegetables upon it, mostly potatoes. But Mrs. Dyer liked string-beans and peas; so they had a few of these, and pumpkins, when the time came; but we have nothing to do with them at present. If I began to tell you what Mrs. Dyer liked, it would take a great while, because there are marrow-squashes and cranberry-beans, though she did not care so much for tomatoes; but vegetables do help out, and don't cost as much as butcher's meat, if you don't keep sheep; but hens Mrs. Dyer did keep. It was the potatoes that were most successful, for it was one summer when everybody's potatoes had failed. They had all kinds of diseases, especially at Spinville, near which Mr. Dyer lived. Some were rotten in the middle, some had specks outside; some were very large and bad, some were small and worse; and in many fields there were none at all. But Mr. Dyer's patch flourished marvellously. So, after he had taken in all he wanted for himself, he told his wife he was going to ask the people of Spinville to come and get what they wanted.

"Now, Mr. Dyer!" said his wife. She did not say much else; but what she meant was, that if he had any potatoes to spare, he had better sell them than give them away. Mr. Dyer was a poor man; why should not he make a little money?

But Mr. Dyer replied that he had no cart and horse to take the potatoes to Spinville with, and no time either. He had agreed to mow the deacon's off-lot, and he was not going to disappoint the deacon, even if he should get a couple of dollars by it; and he wasn't going to let his potatoes rot, when all Spinville was in want of potatoes. So Mr. Dyer set to work, and printed in large letters on a sheet of paper these words: "All persons in want of potatoes, apply to J. Dyer, Cranberry Lane, Wednesday, the fifteenth, after seven o'clock, A.M. Gratis."

The last word was added after Mr. Dyer had pasted the notice against the town hall of Spinville; for so many people came up to bother him with questions as to how much he was going to ask for his potatoes, that he was obliged to add this by way of explanation, or he would never have got to the deacon's off-lot Tuesday morning.

Wednesday morning, Mrs. Dyer sat by the front window, with her darning. She had persuaded Mr. Dyer to wait till Wednesday; for as for having all the people tramping through the yard when the clean clothes were out, she couldn't think of it; and she might as well get through the ironing, then she could have an eye on them. And how provoked they'd all be to come down all that way to Cranberry Hollow, to find only a bin of potatoes to divide among them all.

The little shed was full of potatoes, Mr. Dyer answered. And he had no idea many people would come, just the poorer ones; and as long as he had any potatoes to spare, he was willing they should take them.

But, sure enough, as Mrs. Dyer said, what a procession came! Poor Mrs. Jones's little girl, with a bag; Tom Scraggs, with two baskets; the minister's son, with a wheelbarrow; and even rich Mr. Jones, the selectman, with a horse and cart. Boys and girls, and old women, and middle-sized men, and every kind of a vehicle, from a tin tipcart to Mrs. Stubbs's carry-all.

Well, let them come, thought Mrs. Dyer. It would just show Mr. Dyer she was right, and he didn't often find that out. She should be disturbed by them soon enough when they found out that there was not more than half a potato apiece, and like enough, not that. Pretty business of Mr. Dyer, to take to giving away, when he had not more than enough to put into his own mouth, to say nothing of Jedidiah's! So she went on darning and thinking. What was her surprise, all of a sudden, to hear only shouts of joy as the people returned round the corner of the house! Poor Mrs. Jones's little girl gave a scream of delight as she held up her bag full of potatoes; the minister's son had hard work to push along his full wheelbarrow; rich Mr. Jones was laughing from the top of his piled-up cart; Tom Scraggs was trying to get help in carrying his baskets. Such a laughing, such fun, was never heard in Spinville, which is a sober place. And they all nodded to Mrs. Dyer, and gave shouts for Mr. Dyer, and offered Jedidiah rides in all their carts, those that had them, and asked Mrs. Dyer what they could do for her in Spinville. And Jedidiah tried to tell his mother, through the open window, how the more they took the potatoes out of the bin, the more there were left in it; and how everybody had enough, and went away satisfied, and had filled their pockets; and even one of the boys was planning a quill popgun for sliced potato, such as the worst boys had not dreamed of all summer. He was a bad boy from the Meadow.

"Well, Mr. Dyer!" said Mrs. Dyer, all day, and again when he came home at night.

Of course the Spinville people thought a great deal from this time of Mr. Dyer; and there was a town council held to consider what they should do to express their feelings to him. He had declined six times being made selectman, and he did not want to ring the bell as sexton. There did not seem to be anything in the way of an office they could offer him that he would accept.

At last Mr. Jones suggested that the best way to please the father was to give something to the son. "Something for Jedidiah!" exclaimed Mr. Jones. "The next time I go to New York, I'll go to a toy-shop; I'll buy something for Jedidiah."

So he did. He came home with the Noah's Ark. It was a moderate-sized ark, painted blue, as usual, with red streaks, and a slanting roof, held down with a crooked wire. It was brought to Jedidiah, one evening, just as he was going to bed; so the crooked wire was not lifted, for Mrs. Dyer thought he had better go to bed at his time and get up early and look at his ark. But he could not sleep well, thinking of his ark. It stood by his bedside, and all night long he heard a great racket inside of it. There was a roaring and a grunting and a squeaking,—all kinds of strange noises. In the moonlight he thought he saw the roof move; if the wire had not been so crooked it surely would have opened. But it didn't, not till he took it downstairs, and Mrs. Dyer had got out her ironing-board, that the animals might be spread out upon it; then Jedidiah lifted the roof.

What a commotion there was then! The elephant on the top, and his trunk stretched out; in a minute or two he would have unfastened the wire; the giraffe's long neck was stretched out; one dove flew away directly, and some crows sat on the eaves. Mr. and Mrs. Dyer and Jedidiah started back, while the elephant with his trunk helped out some of the smaller animals, who stepped into rows on the ironing-board as fast as they were taken out.

The cows were mooing, the cats mewing, the dogs barking, the pigs grunting. Presently Noah's head appeared, and he looked round for his wife; and then came Shem and Ham and Japheth with their wives. They helped out some of the birds,—white, with brown spots,—geese, and ducks. It took the elephant and Noah and all his sons to get the horses out, plunging and curvetting as they were. Some sly foxes got out of themselves, leaping from the roof to the back of a kneeling camel.

Jedidiah's eyes sparkled with joy. Mrs. Dyer sat with folded hands, and said, "Why, Mr. Dyer!" And Mr. Dyer occasionally helped a stray donkey, whose legs were caught, or a turkey fluttering on the edge. At last a great roaring and growling was heard at the bottom of the ark. The elephant nodded his trunk to the giraffe; the camel was evidently displeased; Noah and his sons stood together looking up at the roof.

"It's the wild animals," said Jedidiah.

"If they should get out," thought Mrs. Dyer; "all the wild tigers and the lions loose in the house!" And she looked round to see if the closet door were open for a place of retreat.

Mr. Dyer stepped up and shut the roof of the ark. It was in time; for a large bear was standing on his hind legs on the back of a lion, and was looking out. Noah and his family looked much pleased; the elephants waved their trunks with joy; the camels stopped growling.

"I don't wonder they are glad to get out," said Jedidiah. "I do believe they have been treading down those wild animals all night."

Mrs. Dyer wondered what they should do with the rest. Come Tuesday she would want her ironing-board,—perhaps baking-day, to set the pies on.

"They ought to have some houses to live in, and barns," said Jedidiah. Then it was Mr. Dyer had said they could never get them back into the ark; and Jedidiah had said, "We might ask the 'grateful people,'"—for this was the name the inhabitants of Spinville went by in the Dyer family ever since the time of the potatoes.

The story of their coming for the potatoes had been told over and over again; then how the "people" felt so grateful to Mr. Dyer. Mr. Dyer said he was tired of hearing about it. Mrs. Dyer thought if they meant to do anything to let Mr. Dyer see they were grateful, they had better not talk so much about it. But Jedidiah called them the "grateful people;" and it was he that caught the first glimpse of the procession when it came up with the ark, Mr. Jones at the head. He had some faith in them; so it was he that thought there ought to be a village built for Noah and his family; and when Mr. Dyer had some doubts about building it he suggested, "Let's ask the 'grateful people.'"

What they did will be told in another chapter.

II.

ABOUT THE GRATEFUL PEOPLE AND THE WILD BEASTS.

That very afternoon there was a great rush to see Jedidiah's Noah's Ark, and there was immense enthusiasm about it. Some brave ones opened the roof and looked in upon the growling wild animals. The girls liked the lambs the best; the boys were delighted with the foxes that jumped on the edge of the boat that formed the ark.

In a day or two there was a flourishing little village built on a smooth place on the other side of Mr. Dyer's house. The minister's daughter had brought a little toy village she had with red roofs, and one of the men scooped out the houses, which were made of one block of wood, but could now accommodate Noah and his family, and each one picked out a house to match the color of his garments.

Tom Stubbs built a barn of wooden bricks for the larger animals, and Lucy Miles brought a pewter bird-cage, with a door that would open and shut, for the birds. The elephant knocked out a brick with his trunk as soon as he went into the barn, but that made a good window for him to look out of. Jedidiah himself made the loveliest coop for the hen; and the boys had a nice time over a pond they dug in the mud, for the ducks.

Indeed, it occupied Spinville for some time; and Noah, Shem, and Ham did not sit down much, but looked very busy. There was a fence built round the whole village, high enough to keep in the elephants and the giraffes, though they could look over. There was a bit of pasture-land shut in for the cows, who fell to nibbling as soon as they were put in it. A clover-leaf lasted one of the sheep two days. The tinman sent some little tin dippers no bigger than a thimble, and the children were delighted to see the animals drink. The boys handed one of the dippers into the ark for the tigers. The giraffes found a bush just high enough for them to eat from. The doves sat on the eaves of the ark, and Agamemnon brought some pickled olives, as he had no olive-branch for them.

The children were never tired of seeing the camels kneel and rise. They made them carry little burdens,—stones that were to be cleared from the field, chips from the henhouse. Sometimes the camels growled; then the children took off a chip or two from their burdens,—the last ounce, they thought.

The "grateful people" sent a large umbrella, used by the umbrella-maker for a sign, that could be opened over the whole village in case of a rain; and the toy-shop man sent a tin teapot, though Mrs. Dyer did not venture to give Noah and his family any real tea; but it was a very pretty teapot, with a red flower upon it. Mrs. Noah liked it, though it was almost large enough for the whole family to get into.

All this was not the work of a day, by any means. First, all Spinville had to come and look at the things, and then it had to discuss the whole affair. Mrs. Dyer's knitting got on bravely, for so many of her friends came in to sit in her best parlor, and talk it all over. Mrs. Dyer agreed with them; she thought it was all very strange. She should be thankful if only the tigers would never get out. She did not like having tigers running in and out of the house, even if they were no bigger than your thimble. She thought it quite likely some of the boys would let them out some day; but it was no use looking forward. So, day by day, the people came to look at the wonderful village. There was always something new to see. At last, one of the deacons declared Jedidiah ought to charge so much a sight. It was as good a show as the menagerie, any day; and everybody was willing to give ten cents for that, children half-price.

This made great talk. Should Jedidiah charge for the show, or not? Mr. Dyer would have nothing to say about it. Mrs. Dyer thought they might as well; then there would be fewer children in her front yard picking at the currants. At last it was settled that Spinville should pay two cents a sight, children half-price, and strangers could see the village for nothing; but all those who had contributed anything towards the ark should have a right to visit it with their families, without paying. There was a great rush after this to see who was going to pay. It turned out only the schoolmaster's and doctor's families had to buy tickets; and when it came to that, Mr. Dyer said he would not let them pay anything. So Jedidiah did not gain much by it; but he and a few of his friends made some tickets, all the same, printing on them "Noah's Ark. Admittance, two cents; children, half-price;" and a good many children bought tickets for the fun of it.

At last there came a crash. One afternoon, Tim Stubbs, in setting up a new pump, gave a knock to the ark, and sent the whole thing over. The roof snapped open, and out came all the wild beasts. The hyenas laughed, the lions roared, the bears growled, and the tigers leaped about to see whom they could devour; Noah jumped up on top of the pump; the elephant knocked out a side of the barn, to see what was the matter; all the wives ran for the houses, and there was a general confusion. A leopard seized a young chicken. Mrs. Dyer came out with a rolling-pin in her hand. Tim and Tom Stubbs declared they would catch the animals, if Jedidiah would only find something safe to put them in.

"If we only had a cave!" exclaimed Lucy Miles, who had hidden behind the kitchen door.

Tim and Tom Stubbs caught one of the tigers, just as Jedidiah appeared with his mother's bandbox. He had thrown his mother's caps and her Sunday bonnet on the spare-room floor. They shut the tiger up in the bandbox, then found one of the bears climbing up the pump after Noah. Jedidiah brought a strong string, and tied him to a post. All the rest of the boys ran away at first, but ventured to come back and join in the search for the rest of the beasts.

The hunt grew quite exciting. One of the boys, who had read African travels, prepared a leash of twine, and made a lasso, and with this he succeeded in catching the two hyenas. Then no one knew if all the beasts were caught or no. The boy who had read the travels could tell a long list of wild animals that ought to be in the ark. There was the rhinoceros, the hippopotamus, the jaguar; there was the leopard, the panther, the ocelot. Mrs. Dyer put her hands up to her ears in dismay. She could not bear to hear any more of their names; and to think she might meet them any day, coming in at the wood-house door, or running off with one of the chickens!

But the Stubbses thought very likely all these animals never were in this ark at all, though they might have been in the original Noah's Ark. This was only a play ark, after all, and you could not expect to find every animal in it. The minister's wife said she did not know what you should expect. The ark was quite a different one from any she had seen. She had bought them for her children, year in and year out, and she had never seen anything of the sort. You might expect a hippopotamus, or any kind of beast. Those she had bought were always of wood, and the legs broke off easily. You could mend them with Spalding's Glue; but even Spalding was not as good as it used to be, and you could not depend upon it.

Meanwhile the hunt went on. The Spinville people began to be sorry they had ever bought a Noah's Ark. They had expected nothing of the sort. At last the two leopards were found,—beautiful creatures, who lashed their tails wildly; and before long, two hippopotami were discovered in the duck-pond, wallowing in their native element. They were very fierce and wild, and were caught with great difficulty. These were put in the bandbox with the others. It was a strong, old-fashioned box; but it was feared it would not last long for the wild beasts. Jedidiah tied it up with some twine, and it was put for the present in the spare-room closet.

Mrs. Dyer did not sleep well that night, though her doors had been shut all day. She dreamed she heard lions all the night long, and was sure a rhinoceros could get in at the window. Why had Mr. Dyer ever been so generous with his potatoes? Why had he invited all the people to come? Of what use had the

Noah's Ark been? Jedidiah had got along without toys before; now his head was turned. Better for him to amuse himself digging potatoes, or seeing to the squashes, than meddling with the beasts.

And there were the Spinville boys round before breakfast. They were there, indeed, and began again their search for the beasts. The girls sat at the chamber windows, watching the chase. Under a cabbage-leaf, fast asleep, the stray tiger was found. The boy learned in Natural History went over the terrible list of all the fierce animals. "Yes, there were ocelots and cougars and jaguars, peculiarly shy and stealthy in approaching their prey," so the book said. "There was the chibiguasu——" But Jedidiah said he didn't believe *his* Noah cared for such out-of-the-way beasts; they must have come in since his ark. They had enough to do to catch the regular wild animals, and these at last they found in some number. They were all seized, and with difficulty put into a wooden lozenge-box. There was great delight; there must be all; the ark surely could have held no more. Lions, tigers, leopards, panthers, lynxes, wildcats,—all the animals necessary for a respectable ark, all in twos.

But, oh horror! a jaguar was discovered, also, at the last moment just before school. One jaguar, and there must be another somewhere. The one found answered the description completely: "the body yellow, marked with open black figures, considerable variety in the marking." A stray jaguar in Spinville! so fierce a beast! No one could be sure of his footsteps. Noah, his sons and their wives, had not been unmoved. Their satisfaction had been great. They had carried water to the bears, and had looked much pleased; and now they shook their heads at seeing only one jaguar.

"I think they must be all caught but that one jaguar," said Jedidiah. "They look satisfied, and are going about their daily work; and it is time we found some place for the wild beasts. They will come through mother's bandbox before long."

The boys went to school. There was great consultation all that day, which ended in Tom Stubbs bringing a squirrel-cage. It was just the thing, for the wires were near enough to keep the animals in, and everybody could have a look at them. But how were they to be got into the squirrel-cage? There came a new question. Tim Stubbs remembered he had often caught a butterfly under his hat, and a very handsome butterfly, too, and he was sure he had him; but just as he lifted the brim of the hat to show the other fellows that he was really there, the butterfly would be off.

Happily there was no afternoon school, and a grand council of the boys was held, assisted by some of the selectmen. The beasts in the lozenge-box were easily disposed of, for it had a sliding cover, which was dexterously raised high enough to let the beasts all into the squirrel-cage. Then handy Tim

Stubbs punched a hole in the bandbox opposite to the entrance of the squirrel-cage, and one by one the leopards and the rest were allowed to make their way into the wiry prison. The tiger made a dash, but in vain; he was imprisoned like the rest.

This is our last news from Spinville.

It is more than a month since the Spinville stage set out on its weekly trip for that place. It was an old stage; the horses were old, the harness was old, the driver was old. It is not then to be wondered at that in crossing the bridge on the old road, which is so little travelled that it is never kept in repair, the old wheel was caught in a chink between the boards, the old coach tumbled over, the driver was thrown from his seat and broke his leg, the horses fell on their knees, and the whole concern was made a complete wreck.

Now, the stage-driver was the owner of the old coach and team. He had always said the thing did not pay; he would give it all up. Indeed, he only had driven to Spinville once a week to see the folks himself. Nobody ever went there, and nobody ever came away, except once a year Mr. Jones, and he had a team of his own. So there is no communication with Spinville. That a jaguar is loose is the latest news.

XI.

CARRIE'S THREE WISHES.

Carrie Fraser was a great trouble to her mother, because she was always wishing for something she had not got.

"The other girls always have things that I don't," she complained to her mother. Her mother tried to explain to Carrie that she had a great many things the other girls didn't have.

"But they are not always wishing for my things, just as I wish for theirs."

"That is because they are not such 'teasers' as you are," her mother would reply. "You do not hear them from morning till night teasing for things they have not got."

Another thing in Carrie troubled her mother very much. She used a great many extravagant phrases. She was not satisfied with saying even "perfectly lovely," "splendid," "excruciatingly jolly." Her mother might have permitted these terms, and was used to hearing the other girls use them; but Carrie got hold of the strangest expressions and phrases, I am afraid to put them into this story; for every boy and girl is perhaps already too familiar with such, and I might only spread the use of them.

I will mention that "bang-up" and "bumptious," and that class of expressions were her favorites, and the best-educated boy or girl will be able to imagine the rest. This story will show how a careless use of words brought Carrie to grief, and taught her a severe lesson.

One day, as usual, she had been complaining, and wishing she could have everything she wanted. Her mother said: "You remember the old story of the old couple who had their three wishes granted, and how they never got any good from it."

"But that was because they acted like such geese," exclaimed Carrie. "I could never have been so elephantinely idiotic! First, they wasted one wish, for a black pudding."

"That is a sausage," said her mother.

"Yes, they asked for a common, every-day sausage to come down the chimney; then they got into a fight, and wished it would settle on one of their noses; and then they had to waste their last wish, by wishing it off again! It is too bad to have such luck come to such out-and-out idiots."

Mrs. Fraser was just setting out for the village street, to order the dinner. The Governor was expected to pass through the place, and was to be met at the Town Hall. Jimmy, the only son in the family, had gone off to see the show.

"Now, if he were a real, genuine governor," said Carrie, "like a prince in a fairytale, you would go and beseech him to grant your wishes. You would fall on your knees, or something, and he would beg you to rise, and your lovely daughter should have all that she wished."

"I am afraid you are very foolish," sighed Mrs. Fraser; "but I will see the Governor. Perhaps he can advise what is best."

It seemed to Carrie as if her mother were gone a great while. "She might have got six dinners!" she exclaimed to herself. "How tiresome! I wish I had gone down myself, anyway. All the girls and boys have gone, and I might have seen the Governor."

But she passed the time in rocking backward and forward in a rocking-chair; for to her other faults Carrie added that of laziness, and when the other girls had gone down town, and had urged her to go with them, she had been quite too lazy to go for her hat or to hunt up her boot button-hook.

"It seems as if Jimmy might have come back to tell about things," she went on. "Oh dear me! if I had only a chariot and four to go down with, and somebody to dress me and find my boots and my hat and my gloves, then it would have been worth while to go. I mean to make out a list of wishes, in case somebody should grant me the power to have them."

She took out a little blank-book from her pocket, and began to write down:
—

"1. A chariot and four, man to drive, striped afghan, etc.

"2. Maid to find and put on hat, boots, etc.

"3. Plenty of hats, boots, and gloves for the maid to put on, and so that they could be found when wanted."

"That would be bully!" said Carrie, interrupting herself. "If I had gloves in every drawer and on every shelf, I should not have to be looking for them. I might have a hat on every peg in the house except what Jimmy uses. I might have a sack over the back of every chair, and gloves in the pockets of each. The boots could be in each corner of the room and on all the top shelves. But boot-hooks! there's the stunner! Where could one find boot-buttoners enough? They do get out of the way so! I should have six in every drawer, one in each pocket, half a dozen in Mamma's basket, a row on the mantelpiece—on all the mantelpieces. Then perhaps I could do without a maid; at least, save her up till I grow older. Let's see. That makes three wishes. They generally have three. If I strike out the maid, I can think of something else. Suppose I say something to eat, then. Chocolate creams! I never had enough yet."

At this moment Mrs. Fraser returned, looking quite heated and breathless. She had to fling herself into a chair by the window to recover strength enough to speak, and then her words came out in gasps.

Carrie did leave her rocking-chair and tried fanning her mother, for she saw she had something to say.

"What is it? What have you seen? Have you got something slam-bang for me? Is the Governor coming here? Couldn't you raise any dinner?"

Carrie's questions came out so fast that her mother never could have answered them, even with the breath of a Corliss engine; much less, panting as she was now.

"Yes, I saw him; I managed to see him," she gasped out. "The guns were firing, the cannon were booming, the bells were ringing——"

"Oh! I dare say! I dare say!" cried Carrie, eager to hear more. "I could hear them up here. That was not worth going to town for. What did the Governor say?"

"My dear! my dear!" panted Mrs. Fraser, "he said you could have your three wishes."

"What! The chariot and four (that means horses), the maid, and the boot-hooks,—no, the maid was scratched out,—not the chocolates?" asked Carrie, in wonder.

"No, no! I don't know what you mean!" said Mrs. Fraser; "but you can have three wishes; and I have hurried home, for they are to be told as the clock strikes twelve,—one to-day, one to-morrow, one the next day,—the moment the clock strikes, and I am only just in time. You are to wish, and you will have just what you wish."

Both Carrie and her mother looked at the clock. The hand was just approaching twelve. Carrie could hear a little "click" that always came from inside the clock before it struck.

"I have written out my wishes," she hurried to say; "but I don't want the chariot yet, because everybody is coming back from town. And I don't want any more hats and boots just now. But, oh! I do want some chocolate creams, and I wish this room was 'chock full of them.'"

As she spoke the clock struck; and when it stopped she could speak no more, for the room was as full of chocolate creams as it could hold. They came rattling down upon her head, filling in all the crannies of the room. They crowded into her half-open mouth; they filled her clutching hands. Luckily, Mrs. Fraser was sitting near the open window, and the chocolate creams pushed her forward upon the sill. There were two windows looking upon the piazza. One was made of glass doors that were shut; the other, fortunately, was quite low; and Mrs. Fraser seated herself on the edge, and succeeded in passing her feet over to the other side, a torrent of chocolate creams following her as she came. She then turned to see if she could help Carrie. Carrie was trying to eat her way toward the window, and stretched out her arms to her mother, who seized her, and with all her strength pulled her through the window.

"They are bully!" exclaimed Carrie, as soon as she was free. "They are the freshest I ever ate. Golumptious!"

"Oh, Carrie," said her mother, mournfully, "how can you use such expressions now, when you have wasted your opportunity in such an extravagant wish?"

"What! A whole roomful of chocolate creams do you consider a waste?" exclaimed Carrie. "Why, we shall be envied of all our neighbors; and, Mamma, you have been sighing over our expenses, and wishing that Jimmy and I could support you. Do not you see that we can make our fortune with chocolate creams? First, let us eat all we want before telling anybody; then let us give some to choice friends, and we will sell the rest."

All the time she was talking Carrie was putting in her hand for chocolate creams and cramming one after another. Mrs. Fraser, too, did not refuse to taste them. How could they ever get into the parlor again, unless they were eaten up?

"I am sure we can make quite a fortune," Carrie went on. "As soon as Jimmy comes home we can calculate how much it will be. The last time I was in Boston I gave fifteen cents for a quarter of a pound, and there were just thirteen chocolate creams. Now, see. In my two hands I can hold fourteen; now, how many times that do you suppose there are in the room?"

Mrs. Fraser could not think. Carrie was triumphant.

"Jimmy will know how to calculate, for he knows how many feet and inches there are in the room. If not, he can measure by the piazza; and we can row the chocolate creams out, and see how many go to a foot, and then we can easily find out. Of course, we shall sell them cheaper than they do in Boston, and so there will be a rush for them. It will be bully!"

"I am glad we happened to take this rocking-chair out on the piazza this morning," said Mrs. Fraser, languidly seating herself. "I don't see how we shall ever get into the parlor again."

"Jimmy and I will eat our way in fast enough," said Carrie, laughing; and Jimmy at that moment appeared with two boy friends, whom he had brought home to dinner.

They were all delighted when they understood the situation, and had soon eaten a little place by the window, inside the room.

"I quite forgot to buy any dinner," exclaimed Mrs. Fraser, starting up. "I meant to have ordered a leg of mutton as I went down, and now it is too late; and eggs for a pudding. Jimmy will have to go down——"

"Oh, the chocolate creams will do!" exclaimed Carrie. "Don't you see, there's our first saving, and my wish does not turn out so extravagant, after all. The boys will be glad to have chocolate creams for dinner, I'm sure."

The boys all said they would, as far as they could, when their mouths were so full.

"We must put out an advertisement," said Carrie, at last, as soon as she could stop to speak: "'Chocolate creams sold cheap!' I guess we won't give any away. We may as well make all we can. It will be geminy! Suppose we look up some boxes and baskets, Jimmy, to sell them in; and you boys can go to the gate and tell people there are chocolate creams for sale."

But all the boxes and baskets were soon filled, and only a little space made in the room. Jimmy pulled out the other rocking-chair that Carrie had been sitting in, and she rested herself for a while.

"I declare, I never thought before I could eat enough chocolate creams; but they are a trifle cloying."

"My dear," said Mrs. Fraser, "if you had not said 'chock full;' if you had said 'a great many,' or 'a trunkful,' or something of that sort."

"But I meant 'chock full,'" insisted Carrie.

"I did not mean quite up to the ceiling. I didn't suppose that was what 'chock' meant. Now we know."

A great shouting was heard. All the boys of the town were gathering, and quite a crowd of people seemed coming near.

Mrs. Fraser was a widow, and there was no man in the house. Jimmy was the nearest approach to a man that she could depend upon; and here he was, leading a band of boys! She sent one of the boys she knew the best for Mr.

Stetson, the neighboring policeman, who came quickly, having already seen the crowd of boys flocking to the house.

Carrie was trying to sell off her boxes for fifteen, ten, even five cents; but the crowd could not be easily appeased, for the boys could see across the windows the chocolate creams closely packed. "The room is chock full!" they exclaimed.

Mr. Stetson examined the premises. "You'll find it hard work to get them chocolates out in a week, even if you set all the boys on them. I'd advise letting them in one by one to fill their pockets, each to pay a cent."

Even Carrie assented to this, and a line was formed, and boys let in through the window. They ate a way to the door that led into the entry, so that it could be opened and the room could be entered that way. The boys now went in at the window and came out at the door, eating as they went and filling their pockets. Carrie could not but sigh at thought of the Boston chocolates, more than a cent apiece! But the boys ate, and then the girls came and ate; but with night all had to leave, at last. It was possible to shut the window and lock it, and shut the door for the night, after they had gone.

"I don't see why the chocolates should not stay on there weeks and weeks," said Carrie to her mother. "Of course, they won't be so fresh, day after day; but they will be fresher than some in the shops. I'm awfully tired of eating them now, and feel as if I never wanted to see a chocolate cream again; but I suppose I shall feel different after a night's sleep, and I think Mr. Stetson is wrong in advising us to sell them so low."

Mrs. Fraser suggested she should like to go in the parlor to sit.

"But to-morrow is the day of the picnic," said Carrie, "and we shall be out-of-doors anyhow. I will take chocolate creams for my share. But, dear me! my dress is on the sofa,—my best dress. You were putting the ruffles in!"

"I told you, my dear, one of the last things, to take it upstairs," said Mrs. Fraser.

"And there it is, in the furthest corner of the room," exclaimed Carrie, "with all those chocolates scrouching on it. I'll tell you. I'll get Ben Sykes in early. He eats faster than any of the other boys, and he shall eat up toward my dress. He made a great hole in the chocolates this afternoon. I will have him come in early, and we don't go to the picnic till after twelve o'clock."

"And at twelve o'clock you have your second wish," said Mrs. Fraser.

"Yes, Mamma," said Carrie; "and I have already decided what it shall be,— a chariot and four. It will come just in time to take me to the picnic."

"Oh, my dear Carrie," said her mother, "do think what you are planning! Where would you keep your chariot and the four horses?"

"Oh! there will be a man to take care of them," said Carrie; "but I will think about it all night carefully——"

At that very moment she went to sleep.

The next morning early, Carrie was downstairs. She found she could eat a few more chocolate creams, and Jimmy was in the same condition. She proposed to him her plan of keeping the chocolates still for sale, but eating a way to the sofa in the corner, to her best dress.

Ben Sykes came early, and a few of the other boys. The rest were kept at home, because it turned out they had eaten too many and their parents would not let them come.

A good many of the older people came with baskets and boxes, and bought some to carry away, they were so delicious and fresh.

Meanwhile Ben Sykes was eating his way toward the corner. It was very hard making any passage, for as fast as he ate out a place others came tumbling in from the top. Carrie and Jimmy invented "a kind of a tunnel" of chairs and ironing-boards, to keep open the passage; and other boys helped eat, as they were not expected to pay.

But the morning passed on. Mrs. Fraser tried to persuade Carrie to wear another dress; but she had set her mind on this. She had a broad blue sash to wear with it, and the sash would not go with any other dress.

She watched the clock, she watched Ben; she went in under the ironing-boards, to help him eat, although she had begun to loathe the taste of the chocolate creams.

Ben was splendid. He seemed to enjoy more the more he ate. Carrie watched him, as he licked them and ate with glowing eyes.

"Oh, Ben," Carrie suddenly exclaimed, "you can't seem to eat them fast enough. I wish your throat were as long as from one end of this room to the other."

At this moment the clock was striking.

Carrie was ready to scream out her second wish; but she felt herself pushed in a strange way. Ben was on all fours in front of her, and now he pushed her back, back. His neck was so long that while his head was still among the chocolates, at the far corner of the room, his feet were now out of the door.

Carrie stood speechless. She had lost her wish by her foolish exclamation.

The faithful Ben, meanwhile, was flinging something through the opening. It was her dress, and she hurried away to put it on.

When she came down, everybody was looking at Ben. At first he enjoyed his long neck very much. He could stand on the doorstep and put his head far out up in the cherry trees and nip off cherries, which pleased both the boys and himself.

HE ENJOYED HIS LONG NECK VERY MUCH.

Instead of a chariot and four, Carrie went off in an open wagon, with the rest of the girls. It made her feel so to see Ben, with his long neck, that she got her mother's permission to spend the night with the friend in whose grounds the picnic was to be held.

She carried baskets of chocolate creams, and she found numbers of the girls, who had not eaten any, who were delighted with them, and promised to come the next day, to buy and carry away any amount of them. She began to grow more cheerful, though she felt no appetite, and instead of eating everything, as she always did at picnics, she could not even touch Mattie Somers's cream-pie nor Julia Dale's doughnuts. She stayed as late as she could at her friend Mattie's; but she felt she must get home in time for her third wish, at twelve o'clock.

Would it be necessary for her to wish that Ben Sykes's neck should be made shorter? She hoped she might find that it had grown shorter in the night; then she could do as she pleased about her third wish.

She still clung to the desire for the chariot and four. If she had it, she and her mother and Jimmy could get into it and drive far away from everybody,— from Ben Sykes and his long neck, if he still had it,—and never see any of them any more. Still, she would like to show the chariot and four to her friends; and perhaps Ben Sykes would not mind his long neck, and would be glad to keep it and earn money by showing himself at a circus.

So she reached home in the middle of the morning, and found the whole Sykes family there, and Ben, still with his long neck. It seems it had given him great trouble in the night. He had to sleep with his head in the opposite house, because there was not room enough on one floor at home. Mrs. Sykes had not slept a wink, and her husband had been up watching, to see that nobody stepped on Ben's neck. Ben himself appeared in good spirits; but was glad to sit in a high room, where he could support his head.

Carrie suggested her plan that Ben should exhibit himself. He, no doubt, could earn a large sum. But his mother broke out against this. He never could earn enough to pay for what he ate, now his throat was so long. Even before this he could swallow more oatmeal than all the rest of the family put together, and she was sure that now even Mr. Barnum himself could not supply him with food enough. Then she burst into a flood of tears, and said she had always hoped Ben would be her stay and support; and now he could never sleep at home, and everybody looking after him when he went out, and the breakfast he had eaten that very morning was enough for six peoples' dinners.

They were all in the parlor, where the chocolate creams were partially cleared away. They were in a serried mass on two sides of the room, meeting near the centre, with the underground passage, through which Ben had worked his way to Carrie's dress. Mrs. Fraser had organized a band to fill pasteboard boxes, which she had obtained from the village, and she and her friends were filling them, to send away to be sold, as all the inhabitants of the town were now glutted with chocolate creams.

At this moment Carrie heard a click in the clock. She looked at her mother, and as the clock struck she said steadily, "I wish that Ben's neck was all right again."

Nobody heard her, for at that moment Ben Sykes started up, saying: "I'm all right, and I have had enough. Come along home!" And he dragged his family away with him.

Carrie fell into her mother's arms. "I'll never say 'chock full' again!" she cried; "and I'll always be satisfied with what I have got, for I can never forget what I suffered in seeing Ben's long neck!"

XII.

"WHERE CAN THOSE BOYS BE?"

This was the cry in the Wilson family as they sat down to dinner.

"It is odd," said Aunt Harriet. "I have noticed they are usually ready for their dinner. They may be out of the way at other times, but they always turn up at their meals."

"They were here at breakfast," said Jane, the eldest daughter.

"I helped Jack about his Latin before he went to school," said the mother of the family.

"They are probably at the Pentzes'," said Gertrude. "If our boys are not there, the Pentzes are here; and as long as the Pentzes are not here, I suppose our boys are there."

"I should say they were not likely to get so good a dinner at the Pentzes' as we have here," said Aunt Harriet, as a plate was set before her containing her special choice of rare-done beef, mashed potato, stewed celery, and apple-sauce.

"Who are the Pentzes?" said Mr. Wilson, looking round the table to see if everybody was helped.

"He is a painter and glazier," said Aunt Harriet, "and the mother takes in washing."

"They are good boys," said Mrs. Wilson. "Jonas Pentz stands high in his class, and is a great help to our Sam. Don't you remember him? He is the boy that came and spent a night with Sam a week ago. They have their first lesson in 'Cæsar' this afternoon; perhaps they are studying up."

"Jack always has to go where Sam does," said Gertrude.

This was the talk at the Wilsons' table. The subject was much the same at the Pentzes'. There was a large family at the Wilsons'; so there was at the Pentzes'. Mrs. Pentz was ladling out some boiled apple-pudding to a hungry circle round her. But she missed two.

"Where are Jonas and Dick?" she asked.

A clamor of answers came up.

"I saw Jonas and Dick go off with Sam Wilson after school, and Jack

Wilson, and John Stebbins," said Will, one of the small boys.

"You don't think Jonas and Dick both went to dine at the Wilsons'?" said Mrs. Pentz. "I should not like that."

"I dare say they did," said Mary Pentz. "You know the Wilson boys are here half the time, and the other half our boys are at the Wilsons'."

"Still, I don't like their going there for meal-times," said Mrs. Pentz, anxiously.

"Jonas had a new lesson in 'Cæsar,'" said Mary Pentz. "I don't believe they planned to spend much time at dinner."

But at supper-time no boys appeared at the Wilsons'. Mrs. Wilson was anxious. George, the youngest boy of all, said the boys had been home since afternoon school; he had seen Jack in the kitchen with John Stebbins.

"Jack came to me for gingerbread," said Jane, "and I asked him where they had been, and John Stebbins said, with the Pentz boys. He said something about to-morrow being a holiday, and preparing for a lark."

"I don't like their getting all their meals at the Pentzes'," said Mrs. Wilson, "and I don't much like John Stebbins."

Again at the Pentzes' the talk was much the same.

Mary Pentz reported the boys went through their 'Cæsar' recitation well; she had a nod of triumph from Jonas as he walked off with Sam Wilson. "They had their books, so I suppose they are off for study again."

"I don't like their taking two meals a day at the Wilsons'," said Mrs. Pentz.

"There's no school to-morrow," said Mary, "because the new furnace is to be put in. But I dare say the boys, Sam and Jonas, will be studying all the same."

"I hope he won't be out late," said Mrs. Pentz.

"He's more likely to spend the night at the Wilsons'," said Mary. "You know he did a week ago."

"The boys were round here for a candle," said Will.

"Then they do mean to study late," said Mrs. Pentz. "I shall tell him never to do it again; and with Dick, too!"

Mr. Wilson came hurrying home for a late supper, and announced he must go to New York by a late train.

"A good chance for you," he said to his wife, "to go and see your sister.

You won't have more than a day with her, for I shall have to take the night train back, but it will give you a day's talk."

Mrs. Wilson would like to go, but she felt anxious about the boys. "They have not been home for dinner or supper."

"But they came home for gingerbread," said Aunt Harriet. "I suppose they didn't have too hearty a dinner at the Pentzes'."

"Joanna says they went off with a basket packed up for to-morrow," said Gertrude.

"If the Pentzes did not live so far off, I would send up," said Mrs. Wilson.

"They will be in by the time we are off, or soon after," said Mr. Wilson. "It looks like rain, but it won't hurt us."

Mrs. Wilson and he went, but no boys appeared all the evening.

Aunt Harriet, who had not been long in the family, concluded this was the way boys acted.

Jane sat up some time finishing a novel, and hurried off to bed, startled to find it so late, and waking up Gertrude to say, "It is odd those boys have not come home!"

Why hadn't they?

They couldn't.

This is what happened.

Wednesday afternoon, after school, the younger boys had gone to play at the old Wilson house, far away at the other end of the Main Street, beyond the Pentzes'. This was an old deserted mansion, where the Wilsons themselves had lived once upon a time. But it had taken a fortune and two furnaces to warm it in winter, and half a dozen men to keep the garden in order in summer, and it had grown now more fashionable to live at the other end of the town; so the Wilson family had moved down years ago, where the girls could see "the passing" and Mr. Wilson would be near his business. Of late years he had not been able to let the house, and it had been closely shut to keep it from the tramps. The boys had often begged the keys of their father, for they thought it would be such fun to take possession of the old house. But Mr. Wilson said, "No; if a parcel of boys found their way in, all the tramps in the neighborhood would learn how to get in too." Still, it continued the object of the boys' ambition to get into the house, and they were fond of going up to play in the broad grassy space by the side of the house; and they kept good oversight of the apple crop there.

On this Wednesday afternoon they were playing ball there, and lost the ball. It had gone through a ventilation hole into the cellar part of the house.

Now, everybody knows that if a boy loses a ball it must be recovered, especially if he knows where it is. There is not even a woman so stony-hearted but she will let in a troop of muddy-shoed boys through her entry (just washed) if they come to look for a ball, even if it has broken a pane of glass on its way. So the boys got a ladder from the Pentzes', and put it up at one of the windows where the blind was broken. Jack went up the ladder. The slat was off, but not in the right place to open the window. There could not be any harm in breaking off another; then he could reach the middle of the sash and pull up the window. No; it was fastened inside. John Stebbins tried, but it was of no use.

"It would not help if we broke the window by the fastening," said John; "for the shutters are closed inside with old-fashioned inside shutters."

Here was the time to ask for the key. They must have the key to find that ball, and the boys trudged back to meet Sam just going home from the Pentzes'.

But Sam refused to ask for the key again, He didn't want to bother his father so soon, and he didn't want the bother himself. He had his new "Cæsar" lesson to study; to-morrow, after school, he and Jonas would look round at the house, and find some way to recover the ball, for even the stern and studious Sam knew the value of a ball.

So Thursday noon the boys all hurried up to the Wilson house,—Sam, Jonas, and all. They examined it on every side. They came back to the hole where the ball was lost.

"There's the cold-air box," said Jonas. "Could not Dick crawl in?"

Now, Dick was a very small pattern of a boy, indeed, to be still a boy. Really he might crawl into the cold-air box. He tried it! He did get in! He had to squeeze through one part, but worked his way down fairly into the cellar, and screamed out with triumph that he had found the ball close by the hole! But how was Dick to get out again? He declared he could never scramble up. He slipped back as fast as he tried. He would look for the cellar stairs, only it was awful dark except just by the hole. He had a match in his pocket. Jack ran to the Pentzes' and got a candle, and they rolled it in to Dick, and waited anxiously to see where he would turn up next. They heard him, before long, pounding at a door round the corner of the house. He had found the cellar stairs, and a door with bolts and a great rusty key, which he succeeded in turning. The boys pulled at the door and it opened; and there stood Dick with the ball in one hand, picking up the candle with the other!

What a chance to enter the house! Down the cellar stairs, up into the attics! Strange echoes in the great halls, and dark inside; for all the windows were closed and barred,—all but in one room upstairs that opened on a back veranda. It was a warm late-autumn day, and the sun poured down pleasantly upon a seat in the corner of the veranda, where a creeper was shedding its last gay leaves.

"What a place to study!" exclaimed Sam.

"Let's come and spend to-morrow," said John Stebbins; "there's no school."

"No school Friday, on account of the furnace!" exclaimed Jack. "Let's bring a lot of provisions and stay the whole day here."

"We might lay it in to-night," said John Stebbins; "we'll come up after school this afternoon!"

"And I'll tell father about the key this evening," said Sam; "he won't mind, if he finds we have got one."

"Jack and I will see to the provisions," said John Stebbins, "if the rest of you boys will come here as soon as school is over."

It was all so interesting that they were too late for dinners, and had to content themselves with gingerbread as they hurried to school.

"Be sure you tell mother," was Sam's last warning to Jack and John Stebbins, as they parted for their separate schoolrooms.

After school the party hastened to the old house. Sam took the entry key from his pocket and opened the door, leaving Dick to wait for Jack and John Stebbins. They appeared before long with a basket of provisions, and were ready for a feast directly, but delayed for a further examination of the house. It was dark soon, and Sam would not let them stay long in any one room. They must just take a look, and then go home,—no waiting for a feast.

"I'll talk to father this evening, and ask him if we may have it if we keep the whole thing secret."

They fumbled their way down to the lower back door, but could not get it open. It was locked!

"We left the key in the door outside," said Dick, in a low whisper.

"You ninnies!" exclaimed Sam, "somebody saw you and has locked us in."

"Some of the boys, to plague us," said John Stebbins.

"Mighty great secrecy, now," said Sam, "if half the boys in town know we are here. It all comes of that great basket of provisions you saw fit to bring round."

"You'll be glad enough of it," said John Stebbins, "if we have to spend the night here."

"Let's have it now," said Jack.

"We may as well occupy ourselves that way," said Sam, in a resigned tone, "till they choose to let us out."

"Suppose we go up to the room with the bed and the sofa," said John Stebbins; "and we've got a surprise for you. There's a pie,—let's eat that."

They stumbled their way back. The provident John Stebbins had laid in more candles, and they found an old table and had a merry feast.

Sam and Jonas had their books. When Sam had hold of a fresh Latin book he could not keep away from it. Jonas's mind was busy with a new invention. The boys thought he would make his fortune by it. He was determined to invent some use for coal ashes. They were the only things that were not put to some use by his mother in their establishment. He thought he should render a service to mankind if he could do something useful with coal ashes. So he had studied all the chemistry books, and had one or two in his pockets now, and drew out a paper with H O, and other strange letters and figures on it. The other boys after supper busied themselves with arranging the room for a night's sleep.

"It's awful jolly," said Dick. "This bed will hold four of us. I'll sleep across the foot, and Sam shall have the sofa."

But Sam rose up from his study. "I've no notion of spending the night here. The door must be open by this time."

He went to the window that looked out on the veranda. There was a heavy rain-storm; it was pouring hard. It was hard work getting down to the door in the dark. The candle kept going out; and they found the door still locked when they reached it.

"Why not spend the night?" said Jonas. "They'll have got over their worries at home by this time."

"Nobody could come up here to see after us in this rain," said Sam. "I suppose they think that as we have made our bed we may as well sleep in it."

Sleep they did until a late hour in the morning. All the windows but the one upon the veranda closed with shutters. They woke up to find snow and rain together. They went all over the house to find some way of getting out, but doors and windows were well closed.

"It's no use, boys," said Sam. "We've tried it often enough from outside to get in, and now it is as hard to get out. I was always disgusted that the windows were so high from the ground. Anyhow, father or some of the folks will be after us sometime. What was it you told mother?" Sam asked.

John Stebbins had to confess that he had not seen Mrs. Wilson, and indeed had been vague with the information he had left with Jane. "I told them we were with the Pentz boys," he said; "I thought it just as well to keep dark."

"Mighty dark we all of us are!" said Sam, in a rage. He was so angry that John Stebbins began to think he had made Jane understand where they were, and he tried to calm Sam down. Jonas proposed that Dick should be put through the cold-air box again. With a little squeezing from behind he must be able to get through. Everybody but Dick thought it such a nice plan that he was obliged to agree. But what was their horror when they reached the place to find some boards nailed across the outside!

"A regular siege!" said Sam. "Well, if they can stand it I guess we can." His mettle was up. "We'll stay till relief forces come. It is some trick of the boys. Lucky there's no school. They can't hold out long."

"A state of siege! What fun!" cried the boys.

"I only wish we had brought two pies," said John Stebbins. "But there's plenty of gingerbread."

Now they would ransack the house at their leisure. There was light enough in the attics to explore the treasures hidden there. They found old coal-hods for helmets, and warming-pans for fiery steeds, and they had tournaments in the huge halls. They piled up carpets for their comfort in their bedroom,—bits of old carpet,—and Jonas and Sam discovered a pile of old worm-eaten books. The day seemed too short, and the provender lasted well.

The night, however, was not so happy. The candles were growing short and matches fewer. Sam and Jonas had to economize in reading, and told stories instead, and the stories had a tendency to ghosts. Dick and Jack murmured to John Stebbins it was not such fun after all; when, lo! their own talk was interrupted by noises below! A sound of quarrelling voices came from the rooms beneath. Voices of men! They went on tiptoe to the head of the stairs to listen.

Tramps, indeed!

How had they got in? Was it they who had locked the door? Did they come in that way?

"Suppose we go down," said Sam, in a whisper. But John Stebbins and the little boys would not think of it. The men were swearing at each other; there was a jingle of bottles and sound of drinking.

"It's my opinion we had better keep quiet," said Jonas. "It is a poor set, and I don't know what they would do to us if they saw we had found them out and would be likely to tell of them."

So they crept back noiselessly. In a state of siege, indeed! John Stebbins, with help of the others, lifted the sofa across the door and begged Sam to sleep on it. But that night there was not much sleep! The storm continued, snow, hail, and rain, and wind howling against the windows. Toward morning they did fall asleep. It was at a late hour they waked up and went to peer out from the veranda window. There was a policeman passing round the house!

Meanwhile there had been great anxiety at the Wilsons'.

"If it were not for the storm," said Aunt Harriet, "I should send up to the Pentzes' to inquire about those boys."

"I suppose it's the storm that keeps them," said Jane.

"If it were not for the storm," Mrs. Pentz was saying to Mary, "I should like you to go down to the Wilsons' and see what those boys are about."

As to Mrs. Stebbins, John was so seldom at home it did not occur to her to wonder where he was.

But when Saturday morning came, and no boys, Aunt Harriet said, "There's a little lull in the storm. I can't stand it any longer, Jane. I am going to put on my waterproof and go up to the Pentzes'."

"I will go too," said Jane; and Gertrude and George joined the party.

Half-way up the long street they met the Pentz family coming down to make the same inquiries,—Mr. and Mrs. Pentz, Mary, Sophy, Will, and the rest.

"Where are the boys?" was the exclamation as they met half-way between the two houses.

Mr. Johnson, one of the leading men of the town, crossed the street to ask what was the commotion in the two families. "Our boys are missing," said Mr. Pentz. "Five boys!"

"We haven't seen them since Thursday morning," said Aunt Harriet.

"They were at home Thursday afternoon," said Mary Pentz.

"I must speak to the police," said Mr. Pentz.

"He is up at the Wilson House," said Mr. Johnson. "There were tramps in the house there last night, and the police came very near catching them. He found the door unlocked night before last. The tramps kept off that night, but turned up last night in the storm. They have got off, however. There is only one policeman, but we've sworn in a special to keep guard on the house."

"I'll go up and see him," said Mr. Pentz.

"We'll all go up," said Harriet.

"Perhaps the tramps have gone off with the boys," said Gertrude.

Quite a crowd had collected with the party as they moved up the street, and all together came to the front of the house. The policeman was just disappearing round the other side. They turned to the back to meet him, and reached the corner where the veranda looked down upon the yard.

At this moment Mr. and Mrs. Wilson appeared. They had arrived at the station from New York, and heard there the story of the disappearance of the boys, and of tramps in the house. They hastened to the scene, Mrs. Wilson almost distracted, and now stood with the rest of the Wilsons and the Pentzes awaiting the policeman. They heard a cry from above, and looked up to the veranda.

There were all the boys in a row.

XIII.

A PLACE FOR OSCAR.

"I don't like tiresome fables," said Jack, throwing down an old book in which he had been trying to read; "it is so ridiculous making the beasts talk. Of course they never do talk that way, and if they did talk, they would not be giving that kind of advice But then they never did talk. Did you ever hear of a beast talking, Ernest, except in a fable?"

Ernest looked up from his book.

"Why, yes," he said decidedly; "the horses of Achilles talked, don't you remember?"

"Well, that was a kind of fable," said Jack. "Our horses never talked. Bruno comes near it sometimes. But, Hester, don't you think fables are tiresome? They always have a moral tagged on!" he continued, appealing to his older sister; for Ernest proved a poor listener, and was deep in his book again.

"I will tell you a fable about a boy," said Hester, sitting down with her work, "and you shall see."

"But don't let the beasts speak," said Jack, "and don't let the boy give advice!"

"He won't even think of it," said Hester; and she went on.

"Once there was a boy, and his name was Oscar, and he went to a very good school, where he learned to spell and read very well, and do a few sums. But when he had learned about as much as that, he took up a new accomplishment. This was to fling up balls, two at a time, and catch them in his hands. This he could do wonderfully well; but then a great many other boys could. He, however, did it at home; he did it on the sidewalk; he could do it sitting on the very top of a board fence; but he was most proud of doing it in school hours while the teacher was not looking. This grew to be his great ambition. He succeeded once or twice, when she was very busy with a younger class, and once while her back was turned, and she was at the door receiving a visitor.

"But that did not satisfy him: he wanted to be able to do it when she was sitting on her regular seat in front of the platform; and every day he practised, sometimes with one ball and sometimes with another. It took a great deal of his time and all of his attention; and often some of the other boys were marked for laughing when he succeeded. And he had succeeded so well that the teacher had not the slightest idea what they were laughing at.

"All this was very satisfactory to him; but it was not so well for him at the end of the year, because it turned out he was behind-hand in all his studies, and he had to be put down into a lower room. But coming into another room with a fresh teacher, he had to learn his favorite accomplishment all over again. It was difficult, for she was a very rigid teacher, and seemed to have eyes in every hair of her head; and he sat at the other side of the room, so that he had to change hands somehow in throwing the balls and getting them into his desk quick without being seen. But there were a number of younger boys in the room who enjoyed it all very much, so that he was a real hero, and felt himself quite a favorite. He did manage to keep up better in his arithmetic, too, in spite of his having so little time for his books. Perhaps from having to watch the teacher so much, he did learn the things that he heard her repeat over and over again; and then he picked up some knowledge from the other boys. Still, all through his school term, he was sent about more or less from one room to another. The teachers could not quite understand why such a bright-looking boy, who seemed to be always busy with his lessons, was not farther on in his studies.

"So it happened, when they all left school, Oscar was himself surprised to find that the boys of his age were ahead of him in various ways. A large class went on to the high school; but Oscar, as it proved, was not at all fitted.

"And his father took him round from one place to another to try to get some occupation for him. He looked so bright that he was taken for an office-boy here and there; but he never stayed. The fact was, the only thing he could do well was to fling balls up in the air and catch them in turn, without letting them drop to the ground; and this he could only do best on the sly, behind somebody's back. Now this, though entertaining to those who saw it for a little while, did not help on his employers, who wondered why they did not get more work out of Oscar.

"A certain Mr. Spenser, a friend of Oscar's father, asked him to bring his boy round to his office, and he would employ him. 'He will have to do a little drudgery at first, but I think we can promote him soon, if he is faithful.'

"So Oscar went with his father to Mr. Spenser's office. Mr. Spenser started a little when he saw Oscar; but after talking awhile, he went to his table, and took from a drawer two balls. 'My little boy left these here this morning,' he said. 'How long do you think,' turning to Oscar, 'you could keep them up in the air without letting them drop?'

"Oscar was much pleased. Here was his chance; at this office the kind of thing he could do was wanted. So he dexterously took the balls, and flung them up and down, and might have kept at it all the morning but that Mr. Spenser said at last, 'That will do, and it is more than enough.' He said, turning to Oscar's father: 'As soon as I saw your boy I thought I recognized him as a boy I saw one day in the school flinging balls up in the air on the sly behind his teacher's back. I'm sorry to see that he keeps up the art still. But I felt pretty sure that day that he couldn't have learned much else. I should be afraid to take him into my office with a propensity to do things on the sly, for I have other boys that must learn to be busy. Perhaps you can find some other place for Oscar.'

"But Oscar could not find the kind of place.

"His friend, Seth Clayton, had been fond of collecting insects all through his school years. Oscar used to laugh at his boxes full of bugs. But Seth used to study them over, and talk about them with his teacher, who told him all she knew, and helped him to find books about them. And it was when she was leaning over a beautiful specimen of a night-moth that Oscar had performed his most remarkable feat of keeping three balls in the air for a second and a half. This was in their last school year.

"And now, after some years more of study, Seth was appointed to join an expedition to go to South America and look up insects along the Amazon and in Brazil.

"'Just what I should like to do,' said Oscar; for he had studied a little about the geography of South America, and thought it would be fun catching cocoanuts with the help of the monkeys, and have a salary too. 'That is something I really could do,' said Oscar to Seth. But Seth went, and Oscar was left behind.

"Will Leigh had the best chance, perhaps. He used to be a great crony of Oscar. He went through the Latin School, and then to Harvard College. 'He was always burrowing into Latin and Greek,' said Oscar; 'much as ever you could do to get an English word out of him.'

"Well, he was wanted as professor in a Western college; so they sent him for three years to a German university to study up his Hebrew. But he was to travel about Europe first.

"'I wish they would send me,' said Oscar. 'Travelling about Europe is just what I should like, and just what I could do. It is a queer thing that just these fellows that can work hard, and like to work too, get the easiest places, where they have only to lie back and do nothing!'

"Even some of the boys who were behind him in school and below him in

106

lower classes came out ahead. Sol Smith, whom Oscar always thought a stupid dunce, had the place in Mr. Spenser's office that he would have liked.

"'Mr. Spenser took Sol out to his country place in the mountains,' Oscar complained, 'where he has boats and plenty of fishing. I know I could have caught a lot of trout. It is just what I can do. But that stupid Sol, if he looked at a trout, he probably frightened it away.'

"It was just so all along through life. Oscar could not find exactly the place he was fitted for. One of his friends, Tracy, went out West as engineer. 'I could have done that,' said Oscar; 'I could have carried the chain as easy as not. It is a little hard that all the rest of the fellows tumble into these easy places. There's Tracy making money hand over hand.'

"The next he heard of him Tracy was in the legislature. 'That I could do,' said Oscar. 'It is easy enough to go and sit in the legislature, with your hands in your pockets, and vote when your turn comes; or you needn't be there all the time if you don't choose.'

"So they put Oscar up for the legislature; but he lost the vote, because he forgot to sign his name to an important note, in answer to one of his 'constituents.' He tried for Congress, too, but without success. He talked round among his friends about running for President. There was the great White House to live in. He would be willing to stay all summer. He felt he should be the right person, as he had never done anything, and would offend no party.

"But even for President something more is needed than catching half-a-dozen balls without letting them fall to the ground.

"Once, indeed, he had thought of joining a circus; but he could not equal the Chinese juggler with the balls, and it tired him to jump up and down. His father got him the place of janitor at an art building; but he made mistakes in making change for tickets, and put wrong checks on the umbrellas and parasols, so that nobody got the right umbrella. He was really glad when they dismissed him, it tired him so. It was harder work than flinging balls——"

"Look at here, you need not go on," said Jack, interrupting his sister. "I never did it but just once in school, and that was when you happened to come in and speak to Miss Eaton. I was real ashamed that you caught me at it then, and I have never had the balls at school since, or thought of them."

"The beast has spoken," said Ernest, looking up from his book.

Jack made a rush at his brother. "Oh! stop," said Ernest; "let us find out what became of Oscar."

"He has married," said Hester, "and his wife supports him."

XIV.

THE FIRST NEEDLE.

"Have you heard the new invention, my dears,
That a man has invented?" said she.
"It's a stick with an eye,
Through which you can tie
A thread so long, it acts like a thong;
And the men have such fun
To see the thing run!
A firm, strong thread, through that eye at the head,
Is pulled over the edges most craftily,
And makes a beautiful seam to see!"
"What! instead of those wearisome thorns, my dear,
Those wearisome thorns?" cried they.
"The seam we pin,
Driving them in;
But where are they, by the end of the day,
With dancing and jumping and leaps by the sea?
For wintry weather
They won't hold together,
Seal-skins and bear-skins all dropping round,
Off from our shoulders down to the ground.
The thorns, the tiresome thorns, will prick,
But none of them ever consented to stick!
Oh, won't the men let us this new thing use?
If we mend their clothes, they can't refuse.
Ah, to sew up a seam for them to see,—

What a treat, a delightful treat, 't will be!"

"Yes, a nice thing, too, for the babies, my dears,—

But, alas, there is but one!" cried she.

"I saw them passing it round, and then

They said it was only fit for men!

What woman would know

How to make the thing go?

There was not a man so foolish to dream

That any woman could sew up a seam!"

Oh, then there was babbling and screaming, my dears!

"At least they might let us do that!" cried they.

"Let them shout and fight

And kill bears day and night;

We'll leave them their spears and hatchets of stone

If they'll give us this thing for our very own.

It will be like a joy above all we could scheme,

To sit up all night and sew such a seam!"

"Beware! take care!" cried an aged old crone,

"Take care what you promise!" said she.

"At first 't will be fun,

But, in the long run,

You'll wish that the men had let the thing be.

Through this stick with an eye

I look and espy

That for ages and ages you'll sit and you'll sew,

And longer and longer the seams will grow,

And you'll wish you never had asked to sew.

But nought that I say.

Can keep back the day;

For the men will return to their hunting and rowing.

And leave to the women forever the sewing."

Ah! what are the words of an agedcrone,

For all have left her muttering alone;

And the needle and thread they got with such pains.

They forever must keep as dagger and chains.

Lightning Source UK Ltd.
Milton Keynes UK
UKHW041829190822
407575UK00002B/60